DEDICATION

This story is dedicated to all the truth seekers, independent thinkers, and awakened warriors. May courage be your weapon.

The Making of The Elberton Enigma

A Mysterious Adventure

Kevin W. Reese

ISBN-13: 978-0692594780

AUTHORS NOTE

Open your eyes before you die.

CHAPTER 1
THE IDEA

"Mr. Calloway? Excuse me… Mr. Calloway, are you with us today!?"

My head jerked up off my desk as the professor's voice echoed through the classroom. I heard a few students laugh as I looked around not really knowing where I was for a moment.

"Yes…yes Dr. Hickenbottom... I'm here." I replied, still in a daze.

He continued in a displeased tone, "Mr. Calloway, I'd like to see you after class please."

I nodded my head yes.

After Dr. Hickenbottom dismissed us, I walked slowly to the front of the class. Anxiety filled my body as I anticipated a lecture. I'm ashamed that I haven't been doing well this semester. I have aspirations of being a filmmaker and Dr. Hickenbottom's 'Intro to Filmmaking' class should be a priority for me. But last night my roommate Ronnie had some indoor weed with orange hairs in it that he got ahold of. I had never been that high in my life! We smoked a blunt and then had a debate on the topic of religion vs. evolution. About an hour into it, we took bong hits. My mind wandered into the past... and the future. Needless to say, last night I just couldn't sleep. I kind of still feel high today actually.

The professor put his hand on my shoulder and looked me straight in the face.

"Mr. Calloway, I have to say that I am concerned about you. You're one of Ashford University's brightest Communication students. I'd hate to see you throw it away. Dr. Nash informed me that you're not doing well in his script writing class either. I took the liberty of looking at your records. Your transcript reflects that you did well your freshman and sophomore year, so for you to decline as a junior indicates that there's something personal going on with you. If you can't tell, I have a special interest in your success Mr. Calloway. You're very talented."

"Thank you." I replied, feeling humbled.

"I wanted to let you know, I am available if you ever need to talk."

His words moved me. "I appreciate it. I'm just in a funk right now. I will be okay. I promise."

"Okay, well, next class I'm going to be assigning a big project. You need a good grade so you can pass this class. I think it's right up your alley and I would like you to put your all into it. Can you do that Mark?"

"Yes Sir." I replied curiously, "May I ask what it is?"

He paused, and broke into a wide smile. "It's going to be a short documentary."

My face lit up! "Now that I can handle!"

"You've been on me all year to teach something that wasn't under your skill set, well, all those fundamental classes are about to culminate into this project. So now is the time for you to prove that you only slacked on those lessons because you already knew them."

"I got you loud and clear sir." I smirked.

Dr. Hickenbottom nodded and I left the classroom.

On my way back to the dorm, I thought of all the possible documentary topics I could produce. Religion vs. evolution was first on my mind from my convo with Ronnie last night. The AIDS conspiracy was another. I began to get excited at the possibilities as I wondered what the details of the project would be. My whole life I've been fascinated with documentaries, especially on controversial topics. Instead of watching sitcoms and TV dramas I would watch the History and Discovery channels as a kid. This would be the perfect opportunity to show my filmmaking skills. I wanted to prove to myself and Dr. Hickenbottom that I had what it takes.

When I got to my on-campus apartment, my roommate Ronnie was in the kitchen making a sandwich. Ronnie was one of those attention-getting, class clown types. He was loud, outspoken and always came off like he was correct. It took a few months of living together to get used to him, but he grew on me. It's also nice that he is a year older, so he can always buy alcohol for me and the guys.

"Bro, were you as fucked up as I was last night?" He smiled as he spoke loudly.

"Yeah man, those trees were no joke dude, I was barely able to get through my classes today."

"Me neither." He laughed out loud. "I got some more, wanna go take some bong hits?"

I was silent for a second, trying to catch my thoughts.

"Nah, I'm gonna pass. I gotta focus on school man, I need to step my game up." I replied, kind of amped up from Dr. Hickenbottom's pep talk.

Ronnie bit into his sandwich looking at me in awe. "You sure bro? I mean, with everything you went through this summer, I figured taking some edge off would be good." He paused to chew, then began talking with a mouth full of food. "Besides, this type of weed doesn't come through very often. This is like some G4 classified cure your cataract type shit!"

I laughed at his excitement and hand movements, "I'm straight dude." I replied and walked to my room.

Ronnie's comment got me thinking about the summer that just passed. I found out my girlfriend had been seeing another guy. And of course I found out the hard way. I had a heart necklace engraved with our names. When I went to her apartment to surprise her, she was in the parking lot kissing another guy. In an act of rage, I ran up on them and threw the necklace at her and spit on the guy. He hauled off and punched me in the face. I'd love to tell you that we fought and I got the best of him, but the truth is, I was knocked out cold. I woke up in the ER. I lost my girl and pride that day. She must have brought me to the hospital because I woke up with a note next to me from her, saying that she was sorry. She didn't even stick around for me to wake up. What a coward! Still today, I can't figure out what I did wrong to make her do this to me. I thought she loved me. As you can imagine, this incident put me in a funk.

After getting my heart ripped out, it felt good getting back to campus in August to start my junior year. Not being in my home town, and knowing that I didn't have to run into her was a relief. I don't even know how I would act if I ran into them together. I'd probably get knocked out again! When I got back to school, I poured myself into partying. I tried to bag every girl I could at parties to make myself feel better. When I finally did have sex with one of them, I realized it didn't do anything but satisfy my ego. I felt like shit, and that made me drink and smoke even more.

Obviously I've been out of control! My grades have been suffering. Maybe I can put my ego toward something more meaningful? This documentary was a gateway to get me back on track and back to my focus of becoming a filmmaker. I feel confident. I feel alert. It's time for Mark Calloway to shine!

Dr. Hickenbottom's class couldn't have come fast enough. I sat down at a desk in the front row of the classroom, anxiously awaiting the details on the assignment. When Dr. Hickenbottom came in, he smiled at me and seemed satisfied that I was there early and I was alert.

Dr. Hickenbottom was about six foot seven with grey hair and had a big booming voice to go with his large frame. I always joked with him that he should be an announcer for a basketball team or something.

"Okay class, I have a big project that will act as your final for this semester. Each of you will produce, shoot, and edit your own 15-

minute documentary. You can choose any topic you want, as long as it's clean from profanity. You'll be graded on your storytelling ability and production quality. This includes your interview sound bites, your B-roll and your narration. Your post production work will be taken into consideration as well. Be sure to edit precisely and add quality lower third graphics. I trust you all have learned enough this semester to make this production happen. We will watch the short documentaries in class and you will vote on your top three. The best three will be viewed at the university film fest event next semester."

Excitement continued to flow through me as I walked out of class and over to the campus dining hall. I was pretty set on doing my film on the artificial preservatives that food corporations put in their products. I went Vegan last year and became very aware of what I was putting in my body. I stopped eating meat, dairy, and processed foods and felt so much better. I was passionate about it, so I wanted to explore what they do to our bodies. I think there's a conspiracy on why they're in the food in the first place.

I ordered a salad and sat down to eat. From a distance I saw Ronnie. He nodded his head and came over to sit with me. I expressed my enthusiasm over this film project and told him of my desire to explore the food industry. He took a bite of his cheeseburger and shook his head as if to say "No...No...No!"

"Bro... it's been done a million times." Ronnie was very animated when he spoke passionately.

"It's been kilt bro. All you have to do is search your Netflix. There's health films everywhere! Do you really want to do what everyone else is doing?"

I paused. "Well, I hear you, but this is just a school project."

Ronnie's eyebrows went up. "Bro, you just said how important this was to you and your ambitions to be a filmmaker. This is a chance for you to kill two birds with one stone, dude. Make something that will turn into a feature film so you can get it on Netflix. The 15-Minute version can be just for school."

I nodded my head, agreeing with him as he egged me on.

"And, I'll tell ya Bro, I got the most amazing topic," he said with a smile.

"What???"

He continued to chew his food, then after a pause he said, "Did you hear what happened last week in Elberton?"

"No, what?"

He leaned in close to me and lowered his voice, almost as if to speak secretly. "A woman reported that her dog was stolen..."

I cut him off and looked at him with a grin. "Are you serious right now? This is your idea?" I said with a chuckle.

He continued, "No, no, Mark, listen man. She reported the dog stolen, then a few days later the dog returned home. The unusual part is, the dog couldn't bark anymore...like...No noise comes out when it barks bro."

I had a blank stare. "Are you high!?"

Ronnie looked at me with an unusual straight face. "It's in one of those weird magazines at the market, it's on the internet too. I saw it yesterday actually. I meant to bring it up to you. I had a dream about it too! Bro, it's trippy. Everyone is obviously making it out to be a joke, but what are the chances of such an unusual story happening so close to us. I mean Elberton is what...like 2, maybe 3 hours away from Marietta? Bro, you have to do this story. Opportunities like this don't happen every day."

"I see your point, but what's the angle? How can this become a feature film, Ronnie?"

He leaned in again. "By investigating. How did this happen to her dog? Is there a dognapper out there? Did she do experiments herself on the dog? Is she just flat out nuts? We could unravel a mystery that the local news won't touch because it's too weird for them. In fact, I would love to help you, I can be your cameraman.

Let's interview the lady, see where it leads. This is the making of a riveting mystery story. If it doesn't lead anywhere, you have yourself a 15-minute project for class. If it goes further, we have the most amazing documentary ever!"

Ronnie was pretty convincing. Even more importantly, he seemed very serious about it.

"Let's go to the supermarket and get a copy of the Inquirer," he said.

I agreed.

CHAPTER 2

The Headline

We hopped in his car and took off. Another advantage of having Ronnie as a roommate and friend was he had a car. I didn't have one, and he was more than willing to bring me anywhere. He was a very loyal and generous guy. However, his offerings usually included weed.

When we got to the market, he pointed out the magazine at the checkout register. As we waited in the express aisle, I skimmed through the article. It read, *"Witch Casts a Spell on Her Dog?"*. I laughed out loud as I thought of how absurd these magazines will sound just to sell copies.

I read further. Her name was Barbara Blank. She looked to be heavy set with dark, black hair. The article stated that she was a 62 year old widow that lived in a farmhouse in Elberton on a few acres of land. The article angled the story as if this lady was a witch of some sort. According to the article, she's an open follower of the Wicca religion and she worshipped the devil.

I took my face out of the magazine and looked up at Ronnie as he paid the clerk. He stared back at me with his eyebrows raised and said, "I told you bro. Listen to me, I'm a genius."

I nodded. "Let's interview the writer of this article first. He already did some investigative work, so it makes sense to start there." I said.

Ronnie pumped his fist, "I'm following your lead bro. You're the boss."

I took out a notepad in the car and started to take some pre-production notes. I listed all the interviews that needed to be booked. First would be the writer of the magazine article. Second would be any others that know Barbara Blank. Then we would interview Blank herself. I figured these three interviews would be enough for the 15-minute assignment at the very least. I then started to draft questions that can be asked to the magazine writer.

When I got back to the apartment, I started researching how to find the writer of the article. It wasn't long before I came up with the main number to the Inquirer magazine. I was thrilled to find out that it was right here in Atlanta, about a half hour from campus.

Ronnie was in his room down the hall. "I'm gonna call now!" I yelled.

He yelled back. "Hey man, you want a bong hit before you call!?"

I shook my head. "No!" I couldn't help but chuckle after his question.

"Awwwwwwww Shit! Someone's focused!" He yelled back.

I was focused, I felt alert and alive. As I dialed the magazine number I realized that this is what I wanted to do for a living one day. Tell stories through video. The secretary answered and I asked for Matt Cardona Jr. After about a 2 minute wait, he answered but seemed in a rush.

"This is Matt."

"Hi Matt, My name is Mark Calloway and I am currently producing a documentary on Barbara Blank and her dog. I was wondering if I could interview you to get some insight on the situation."

"No...No thank you, this doesn't sound like something I would be interested in. But thanks for thinking of me," he replied, speaking abruptly. I needed to think fast, as he was on the verge of hanging up.

Words came flying out of my mouth. "Listen, I really need this for school. I am an upcoming filmmaker and this is a big project for class. This story has intrigued me and I believe there is more story to uncover. Would you be able to just give me ten minutes of your time?"

He paused, then sighed. "The ol' I'm a student trick huh?" He chuckled, "Alright, I remember being a student once. How about next Tuesday at 3 PM at my office."

"Yes, that would be great, Matt. Thank You."

Before hanging up he said, "Listen kid, this is a weird mysterious story, I hope you're only gonna touch the surface, cause you may not like what you find below it."

We hung up and I felt a rush come over me. My first documentary interview was booked. Oh Shit, I have to call the Communications Department to book the camera, mics and get some mini DV tapes. I felt overwhelmed.

At that moment, Ronnie came walking in with smoke pouring out of his nose and mouth. "Soooo?" He asked.

"We're all set for next Tuesday at 3 PM." I said.

He smiled as he took another hit from his bowl. "Let's do it bro!" He replied as he halfway choked on the smoke.

We got to the Atlanta office building about 30 minutes early. The secretary showed us to the company conference room where we could set up shop. Matt came walking in 15 minutes past 3PM and shook our hands. I clipped the lavalier mic on his shirt and did a quick sound check. My heart was pounding, as this was my first time outside of class doing an interview with a stranger. I turned on the lights and signaled to Ronnie to turn the camera on.

Ronnie hit record…

ME: So how were you informed about this incident with Mrs. Blank and her dog?

MATT: A tip came in. I can't say from who, but I can tell you that it had to do with Mrs. Blank's second report to the police about the dog's barking situation.

ME: Did you meet with Mrs. Blank?

MATT: No, I spoke to her on the phone.

ME: How were you able to report her living on farmland and her following the Wicca religion?

MATT: We did some research and found out where she frequently goes to breakfast in her town. I spoke to a waitress who knows her from her dinner visits. She provided us with the details of Mrs. Blank's living situation and religion. I guess people misunderstand the religion so they stereotype her in town. Actually, some even stay away from her or criticize her to her face. My understanding is that she is a sort of a recluse and stays in her house a lot. She lives alone with her dog.

ME: Do you know when and how her husband died?

MATT: I don't know the details. All I know is it happened on her property.

ME: What do you make of the dog not barking anymore?

MATT: I think it's the strangest thing I've ever heard, and I've heard some weird things here at this magazine. When word spread around town of the situation, people instantly figured she casted a spell or was experimenting with a spell and that's how it happened. Black magic or something I guess.

ME: So that's why you ran with the headline and the hook of the story?

MATT: Yes

ME: How was your phone conversation with Mrs. Blank?

MATT: It was...different.

ME: How so?

MATT: She seemed spooked by it. She wanted to get her story out because the police were not able to do anything about it. She really seemed to want answers. The dog was apparently stolen or ran away and a few days later showed back up on her porch. And as we know, it no longer makes a barking noise, but still performs the act of barking.

ME: So...what do you make of all this?

MATT: It's just flat out strange. I reported the story, but now it's over for me. I'm running with a new UFO sighting in Hartford now.

ME: Okay, thank you for participating.

As we turned the camera off and started to break the equipment down, I turned to Matt. "I'm wondering if you can tell me what diner she goes to?"

Matt looked at me intensely. "You're really going to pursue this huh? It seems like more than a school project to you, buddy." He shook his head again, "It's Clifford's Diner on Marina Road in Elberton. The waitress I spoke to was named Victoria Guerrero. That's all I can give you, kid."

"Thank you," I replied. "All I need now is a few B-roll shots of you at your desk making phone calls and such."

As we pulled out of the parking lot Ronnie said to me, "Bro, you really went for it at the end there. You're an investigative reporter now!" He laughed out loud.

I replied. "Yeah, I mean, we drove here, might as well swing for the fence. He didn't give great sound bites. I don't even know what I'll be able to use when I go to edit actually. But, he did lead us to Victoria Guerrero."

CHAPTER 3

The Rumor

A few days later, we arrived at the diner in Elberton to interview Victoria. I was thrilled that she agreed to do it when I called. We walked into the diner and asked for her. The hostess pointed her out. My heart stopped! She was beautiful! She looked to be in her early 20's with long dark hair, pretty brown eyes, with a petite build. She had all the curves a guy could desire! I saw those sparkling Latina eyes from 30 feet away. Ronnie nudged me with his elbow alluding to her sex appeal. She came over to us, introduced herself and asked if we can do the interview outside. I agreed.

Ronnie and I set up outside, as it was a beautiful April day. She came out and we mic'd her and did a quick sound check. It was time to begin...

ME: So Victoria, how do you know Mrs. Blank?

VICTORIA: Well, she comes into the diner a few times a month. I've been working here for almost two years and have served her many times. She's a very sweet lady.

ME: Can you tell me more about her? Is she talkative? What's her personality like? Did you know she follows the Wicca religion? Does she talk about it?

VICTORIA: Mrs. Blank always remembers my name and tips very well. I heard she follows Wicca because people talk behind her back and are creeped out by it. But she never speaks of it and if no one told me, I would have no idea. She does seem to be an inward individual, doesn't share too much. Although one time she spoke of her husband and his death...

ME: How did this come about? What happened to her husband?

VICTORIA: Well, one time, I brought her a Mexican omelet that she ordered, and when I brought it to her table she told me that it was her husband's favorite breakfast. She informed me that she orders it every year on the anniversary of his passing. I was heartbroken when she told me this. I put my hand on her shoulder and told her that I'm sure he was a lovely man. She looked up at me and told me that he was a great man whom was taken too soon. She began to tear up. It was heart-wrenching.

She sighed...and started to get misty-eyed herself. Ronnie and I glanced at each other wondering what was coming. Victoria continued...

VICTORIA: She told me that one day he was out back in the yard cutting down some small trees and she heard a scream. When she ran out back he was laying there with his head separated from his body. She said the police thought that he accidentally cut himself with the chainsaw he was using. It's an awful awful story. Oh my goodness, you guys got my mascara running over here."

I looked at Ronnie and the look on his face said to stop the interview. I agreed in my head.

"Okay Victoria thank you." Ronnie turned the camera off as I went to unmic her.

She said. "I'm sorry I got emotional, it's just a horribly sad story."

"I totally understand." I replied.

As I was taking her mic off, we made eye contact at a close range. She unexpectedly hugged me. I could feel warmth of energy flow through me as we embraced. She pulled away and looked me in the eye and said, "I really hope you portray her in a nice light. Mrs. Blank is a nice lady and she has been through so much. I can't imagine what's going through her mind after this dog incident. Not to mention, the town is consistently talking about her behind her back. It's disgusting. People can be so cruel."

I nodded my head to say yes as I smiled at her. There was a

magnetic pull it felt like, and I just wanted to kiss her! We said our goodbyes and I got some B-roll footage of the diner.

In the car on our way back to campus, all I could think about was this horrible picture of Mr. Blank's head being cut off by a chain saw. Ronnie was abnormally quiet.

"So what are you thinking about?" I asked him.

He glanced over at me real quick before looking back to the road.

"Bro, it doesn't make any sense to me. There's no time to scream when your head is being cut off, especially with a chainsaw. A chainsaw would go through you pretty quick. One swoop maybe even. Your voice box and vocal cords would be severed almost instantly right?"

I thought about it. "Yeah, that sounds about right." I replied.

"I think it's time to schedule the big one. Time to interview Mrs....."

I cut Ronnie off. "Not yet. We should talk to the cop that was called to the scene of the dog incident first."

"Ahhhh good thinking bro." Ronnie replied. "By the way, I think this Victoria chick likes you. When you were taking her mic off, I felt uncomfortable, like I walked in on my Dad watching porn or something." He laughed out loud.

I smirked.

CHAPTER 4

The Gold

I ran to Ronnie's room in amazement. When I got to the door, there was a room full of smoke. I shouldn't be surprised.

"What's up bro? Want a hit?" He said with a cheesy grin.

"No." I replied, "You'll never guess what happened. I did some research on Mrs. Blank's report of the dog incident and guess what? The cop that was called to the scene and handled the case..." Ronnie stared at me with curiosity.

"Come to find out, the cop was let go from the force!"

"What!?" Ronnie yelled out. "Why!?"

"I don't know dude, but we need to find out." I replied.

I spent the next few hours trying to find Officer Ritter. Finally I got ahold of him and he agreed to do an interview. We set up the interview for the following evening at the library where I reserved a study room.

We met Officer Ritter at the Library. He looked to be in his late 20's or early 30's. I mic'd him up and began…

ME: So, Officer Ritter…." He interrupted.

RITTER: Please call me Sylvester."

ME: Okay, Sylvester...what were your thoughts and reaction when you got to the scene of the dog incident at Mrs. Blank's house?

RITTER: Ummmmm….It was strange. I'd never gotten a call like that before.

Sylvester took a long pause, then continued.

RITTER: In fact, none of the boys had ever experienced something like that. She reported the dog missing with the local shelters and the Humane Society first. And then called us when the dog came back a few days later and...You know...didn't bark anymore. Mrs. Blank was shaken up and spooked out. She had tears in her eyes as she explained to me the situation and her hands trembled. I thought I was wasting my time when I got to the house. I thought maybe even the boys were ribbing me.

Sylvester looked as though he was staring into space. He continued.

RITTER: Then it happened...the dog started barking...and...No noise came out. I was shocked. Like, forget hearing about it... Seeing it with your own eyes creates a totally different emotion.

ME: What do you think caused it?"

RITTER: I'm not completely sure. I encouraged her to take the dog to the vet. The only thing I could think of is someone with surgical experience kidnapped the dog and did a surgery to take the vocal cords out? Maybe they were sick of the dog barking? I honestly didn't know what to tell her.

ME: Do you mind telling me why you got fired?

RITTER: Well, when I got back to the station, I wrote the report as usual. But the incident stayed on my mind for the next few days. The curiosity was a monkey on my back I guess you could say. I decided to stop in to Mrs. Blank's house randomly. She was actually happy to see me. She kept insisting that I stayed for lunch. Of course, I declined. I asked if I could look at the property. She was all for it.

ME: What happened next?

RITTER: I found some gold. Literally. There was a huge golden nugget out back sticking out of the dirt. It was about the size of my fist. I mean, it must've been worth a few hundred grand. When I got back and told Mrs. Blank, she explained that her late husband used to spend time out back and had found gold in the past. I asked her if I could bring it in as evidence and get an assessment on it. She agreed.

ME: You found gold?

RITTER: Yes sir, and while I was out there, I heard an owl. Funny thing is, it was midday. It was very creepy and I had a gut feeling to leave. Back at the station, I went to the captain and asked to do more work on the case. I was very persistent about it. The curiosity was killing me. It wasn't but a day and a half later they fired me for trespassing and stealing. They said I went to Mrs. Blank's unannounced and left with something of value.

ME: Why do you think you got fired Sylvester?

RITTER: I'm a young guy on the force. I think someone saw how eager I was and didn't want me snooping around. I probably shouldn't even be talking to you on camera.

Sylvester shrugged. After pausing for a while he continued.

RITTER: I don't know... I guess I went too far by just dropping in, but I was drawn to it. There's something about this story that makes you so damn curious. I'm just thirsty for answers on this one. I'm curious to see what you guys dig up for your documentary.

ME: Where does Wicca come in to all this? Did Mrs. Blank discuss her religion at all?

Sylvester raised his eyebrows in confusion.

RITTER: No, I didn't hear anything about that.

On the car ride back to campus, Ronnie was spooked.

"Bro, Bro, Bro...What the fuck!? Okay, you got gold in the backyard of a widowed witch whose dog mysteriously can't make noise anymore after being kidnapped!? And oh by the way, her husband's head was cut off in the back fucking yard!? Then.... the young ambitious cop on the case was fired?! Okay, okay, okay! I want my mommy now!"

I chuckled. "Calm down Ronnie, we're unraveling a mystery. Isn't this what you wanted?"

Ronnie glanced at me. "Yeah well, it's getting a little weird and creepy now."

I glanced back. "You may want to get some really good weed, because it's time for the big one now."

He shook his head and sighed. "I had a feeling you were going to say that."

CHAPTER 5

The Anxiety

I stared at the phone... it seemed like for hours. Yet, when I glanced at the clock it had only been about 3 minutes. I felt my heart rate speed up and I noticed that my hands were clammy. Ronnie looked at me leaning up against my door in my room as I sat at my desk. I had just found Mrs. Blank's phone number but was having trouble dialing it.

"You okay bro? You look like you're about to puke."

I looked up at him. "Yeah, I think so. I'm just coming to a few realizations right now." I replied.

He softly spoke. "Like what?"

"For one, if she doesn't agree to do this interview, then we just did all that work for nothing. I mean, I could squeeze something out of the footage for the sake of my class project, but the Netflix dream would be shattered."

"That's a good point," he replied.

"But besides that pressure, there's also the fear of the unknown. I mean, what are we getting ourselves into? Do you think this is what Matt Cardona meant? Do you think maybe he did more investigating then he led on to... and got scared away?" I looked up with my eyebrows raised.

Ronnie shrugged. "Listen bro, we gotta see this thing through. I'm creeped out too but this seems to be our purpose now. Our path. It's time to dial that number."

The phone rang 3 times and then a woman picked up.

"Hello."

"Yes hi, I'm looking for Barbara Blank please."

"Yes, this is she."

I felt my voice shake. "Hello Mrs. Blank. My name is Mark Calloway and I'm currently producing a documentary on the incident with your dog. It was a very intriguing story to us and I thought it was worth telling."

"Oh, that's great. I've been wanting to get my story out. You know, nobody seems to believe me," she sighed. "They're all just so darn scared of me."

"This is an opportunity that we want to provide you with," I said with more confidence. "How would you like to set up an interview this Friday?"

"Oh I would like that, however, I am taking my dog to the vet that day and it might be a little emotionally draining for me. I don't know what type of news I'm going to receive."

I replied. "I totally understand." I paused as my mind was turning. All of a sudden, an idea came flooding in. "Mrs. Blank, actually, would we be able to shoot your appointment with the vet? That would add a lot to the film and then maybe we can do the interview the next day?

Ronnie looked at me in shock and excitement at my idea.

She replied, "Yes, that is very doable."

She gave me the address to the house and the vet, along with the times. And there you have it. A two for one.

After I hung up the phone Ronnie gave me a fist bump to say good job.

"We're gonna have to crash at a hotel Friday night, it doesn't make sense to drive 3 hours there and then 3 hours back twice," he noted.

"Alright." I said. "We have a few days to prepare. Why don't you book the room close by and I'll prepare the questions for the vet and Mrs. Blank." He nodded his head yes.

The next day I sat in Dr. Hickenbottom's class and couldn't wait for it to be over. I felt like I needed to put him in the loop. When class ended I walked up to him. He looked happy to see me coming to talk to him.

"Mr. Calloway. How's your documentary going?"

"Interesting...Yeah, interesting is the best word I can use."

"Oh yeah?" He replied. "Fill me in."

"Did you hear of the story about the witch in Elberton whose dog went missing, then came back and couldn't bark anymore?"

"Aaaaaaaah, yeah.... I saw the headline in one of those magazines I believe."

"Well, that's the topic I'm covering." I felt compelled to be dramatic so I used the word 'witch' instead of 'Mrs. Blank', assuming he didn't know her name.

"So far... I have interviewed the man who wrote the story in the magazine, who oh by the way, seemed to want nothing to do with it. A waitress that knows the witch and also informed me the witch's husband's head was cut off in her backyard. A police officer who was on the case, but was fired afterwards for stealing gold from her property. And this weekend I'm interviewing the witch herself and shooting her dog's veterinarian appointment. I have no idea what to expect next."

Dr. Hickenbottom stared at me intensely. "Well, interesting certainly is a good description."

I shook my head up and down.

The Professor continued, "Mark, I salute your effort. But you don't have to go this far. I mean, you could have done a 15-Minute documentary on our campus cafeteria if you wanted. You are clearly overachieving on the journalism side of the project, which is honorable. I must ask, do you feel overwhelmed doing all of this research? Do you feel like you're in over your head? And most importantly, are you scared? I mean, a man's head got cut off and a dog doesn't bark anymore. That's some pretty unusual stuff."

"No." I replied. "The work isn't the problem. I've been doing well in my bookings, interviews, and B-roll footage. I have an idea how I want to edit it when I go to post-production. It's more so the topic that is a little creepy. We're unraveling a mystery... I guess you can say. Yes, I'm creeped out and a little scared sir."

Dr. Hickenbottom nodded his head. "Yes, it does sound as though that's what's happening. Does it feel like this is your purpose now?"

"Yes," I replied.

"Then there you go. Always follow your gut feeling. That's your master. Your soul. Your spirit, Mark. Maybe you're meant to unravel this story? Be aware, when you unravel a story, things happen that can change your thinking forever. It's like a soldier in the field of battle that sees and hears things unimaginable to a regular citizen. You must accept this now. Acceptance is powerful Mr. Calloway. For if you accept what can happen going into the situation, you cannot be shocked later. If it gets to be too much, then pull back. Pump the breaks. Then again, if you pull back, you will always wonder 'what if' right? But remember, you're in control. You have free will Mark."

CHAPTER 6

The Dog

We pulled up to the veterinarian's office and saw Mrs. Blank standing in the parking lot with her dog on a leash. Ronnie and I glanced at each other, showing our uncertainty of the situation. We walked over to her, and the dog greeted us in hyper doggie fashion. He was a yellow Labrador that looked to be around 60 pounds. The hyper dog licked, sniffed, and leaned up against us and we both noticed that there was no noise coming out at all.

"Hello Mrs. Blank. I am Mark and this is Ronnie," I said as I shook her hand.

"Hello boys," she replied, "You know, film project aside, it is nice to have someone here with me to go through this experience."

Ronnie jumped in, "Mrs. Blank it's our pleasure. I'm gonna run back to the car and get our equipment."

Here I was, all alone with the town witch. She walked with a cane and looked to be about 5 feet tall with short, jet black hair. She spoke very nasally and softly. I noticed almost no inflections in her cadence. She grinned strangely at me.

"You know I had a son your age. What are you about twenty-one?" She asked.

"Almost, I'll be twenty-one this summer." I hesitated, but couldn't ignore her statement about having a son in past tense.

I bent down to pet and play with the dog. "I'm sorry, you just mentioned a son. May I ask what happened to him?"

She looked up toward the sky and sighed. "Oh he's dead now...He witnessed an accident that his father had. He was pretty traumatized. I suppose seeing your father die in front of you would do that. He ended up getting addicted to alcohol and pills. The work of the devil I tell ya. One day, he overdosed and met his demise. After my husband and son passed, I bought Damian as a 6 week old puppy. He's been my best friend over the past four years.

She looked back down at me and the dog and started petting him too.

"He's a really good boy. Aren't you Damian? You're Mommy's little angel aren't you?"

I couldn't believe what I was hearing. How much had this woman been through? And what did she mean by the devil? Or was I just looking into it too much? I felt as though every corner we made, there would be another strange tragedy. I didn't know what to say, so I kept it standard.

"I'm very sorry to hear that."

She replied, "So, I guess we should go inside and see what this vet is going to say, huh?"

The veterinarian would not grant us access for Mrs. Blank's appointment. However, he did agree to give us an interview afterwards. So Ronnie and I shot some quick B-roll footage of Mrs. Blank and her dog in the waiting room, then we set up in an empty office that the secretary directed us toward.

As we set up our equipment, the secretary asked a question.

"So...I heard about this story on the internet. What have you guys discovered so far about it?"

Ronnie jumped in with a smile, "Ahhhhh, you're going to have to wait till it premiers on Netflix," he said with cockiness. The secretary just smirked.

About 45 Minutes later the vet came in and introduced himself. We mic'd him and did a quick sound check. And Ronnie hit record...

ME: So Dr. Bollea, What was the result of your examination on Damien?

DR. BOLLEA: Damien is a very healthy and happy dog. However, the x-ray reveals that his larynx and vocal cords have been removed, and this takes away his ability to make sounds from his mouth which includes barking. It's a procedure called a Vocal Cord Cordectomy."

ME: So you're saying that there was a surgery done on the dog?

DR. BOLLEA: I don't know how to answer that absolutely. The assumption is yes, however, there are no signs of an incision anywhere on the dog's body. Yet... the larynx and vocal cords have been delicately and precisely removed from Damien as if a professional performed a surgery. I double-checked his records and the last time we saw Damien, everything was intact."

ME: Do you have any...any ideas on how something like this could have happened?

The look on the Vet's face was of awe.

DR. BOLLEA: No. I have never seen or heard of such a thing.

He paused and shook his head.

DR. BOLLEA: I don't know what else to say. It's unexplainable.

We packed up our equipment and headed to the car. Mrs. Blank was waiting for us.

"You have my address right?" She asked.

"Yes ma'am, we will be there tomorrow at noon." I replied.

She went on. "Okay, I will make some stew and biscuits. You boys need your energy."

Ronnie and I got in the car and looked at each other.

Ronnie broke silence first. "I can't wait to get to that hotel bed. I need my sleep bro." He paused, "Tomorrow... we have lunch with a witch," he smirked, "And then you my friend...you have to give the best interview of your life."

CHAPTER 7

The B-Roll

Ronnie and I sat at Mrs. Blank's table waiting to be served as Damien laid at Ronnie's feet.

"I think he likes you." I said with a smile.

Mrs. Blank came from the kitchen with a big pot of stew.

"Oh I'm a Vegan Mrs. Blank so I'll pass on the stew, but these biscuits look great," I said.

She looked at me irritated. "I wish you had told me that, I would have made you something else."

"No no." I said. "That's fine. No worries Mrs. Blank."

"You eat meat, right Ronnie?" She asked.

"Yes, Ma'am. I'm a carnivore," he replied with a goofy smile.

"Good, good," she said as she served him.

He began eating. "This is very tasty, what kind of stew is it?" Ronnie asked.

"It's called German Hasenpfeffer. It's made of potatoes, peppers, onions, parsnips and rabbit marinated in vinegar," she replied.

I looked up from eating my biscuit. Ronnie kept his face down at the stew, probably not wanting to look up and show the reaction on his face.

"Rabbit? I didn't know they sold rabbit meat. Where do you buy that?" I asked.

"Ohhhh I don't. I breed rabbits out back," she said.

Ronnie stayed silent, actually admiring the taste of the meat. But I was curious, so I asked how the process works.

She was happy to explain. "When we moved here in the early 1990's, we had sheep, goats and chickens. My husband taught me how to take care of them and properly butcher. When he passed away, I couldn't maintain the farm but wanted good quality meat. Well, I discovered rabbit. It's a high quality meat and the fur is worth good money. They are really easy to maintain. They only eat leafy clover hay and alfalfa. I have a bunch of hutches out back."

I thought of the popular saying. "So I'm assuming they multiply fast huh?" I asked.

"Oh yeah," she said, "I originally started with 3 — a young buck 9 months old and 2 does of the same age. The following month I had 17 bunnies. I actually sell the meat and fur to a market a few towns over and that helps pay the bills."

"That's very interesting!" I said. The thought crossed my mind of this little witch chopping the heads off of living rabbits as she smiled and laughed. I wanted to ask how she can stand to kill these cute little creatures, but didn't think it was appropriate.

"This is some damn good meat!" Ronnie blurted out.

"Thank You Ronnie. I'll tell ya, it's nice having guests. I don't get to cook for anyone these days. No one comes and visits me," she replied sadly.

"Mrs. Blank, after lunch we will need to shoot some B-roll of your property." I said, shifting the conversation to business.

"Sure, whatever you need," she replied. "That gives me time to clean up before our interview."

Ronnie and I were out front shooting footage of the house. It was an older style farm house that you could tell was built in the late 1800's, maybe early 1900's at best. It was a grayish color with a wraparound porch. We scanned the area to capture the scene. Mrs. Blank's house was off of a dirt road surrounded by woods. The closest neighboring house was a good quarter mile up the road.

"So, was the rabbit really good or were you just being courteous?" I asked Ronnie.

"Nah bro, it was really good. Tasted similar to chicken, but more firm with a greater aftertaste."

"You didn't mind eating it?" I asked.

He took his eye away from the video camera to glance at me. "Are you gonna to give me a lecture on how meat gives your cancer? Or are you going with the poor innocent animal was murdered speech?"

"No. Not today," I said with a smirk.

He fired back, "You need to be worried about this interview. What's your first question gonna be bro?"

"I'm thinking about addressing the elephant in the room right away." I replied.

"You're just gonna ask her if she's a witch?" He asked.

"Might as well get it out of the way."

We started walking to the back yard. It was huge. It had to be two acres give or take. There were a few barns and an empty chicken coop. We walked past the rabbit hutches and stared at these cute little animals as some slept, some played, and some ate.

Ronnie looked up at me and shook his head. "Okay, now I'm starting to feel bad."

We walked further away from the house and deeper onto the

property. Ronnie turned around and got footage of the back of the house from the distance. As he did, I continued walking about 30 feet ahead. There was a brush of shrubs and trees towards the end. I wondered where the property stopped. Then I heard something.

"Hey Ronnie," I called to him, "Do you hear that!?"

"What... the owl?!" He yelled over.

I replied. "The owl? I didn't hear no owl!"

He caught up. "Oh, you mean the water? Yeah I hear that bro. It's coming from behind the brush."

We walked through the brush. It was thick, and occasionally we got pricked with a thorn. On the other side was a beautiful stream that glowed unlike any water I'd ever seen. The flowing stream looked to be only about 3 feet in width and a few feet deep. It was surrounded by two slightly steep small hills of grass. About 30 Feet to the left where we were positioned was a cave-like tunnel. The top of the tunnel acted as a small bridge so you could cross the stream without having to jump over it. I couldn't really see much down the tunnel as it was dark, but you could tell that it went downward. I moved to my left to see what was on the other side of the tunnel bridge. It was more brush on a hill with no sign of the stream continuing. Clearly, the stream goes underground and downward. It was a beautiful scenic view. Ronnie took footage of it just in case we needed it.

All of a sudden we heard Mrs. Blank yelling for us from a distance.

"Boys!? Boys!?"

"We're right here, Mrs. Blank!" I yelled, as we started making our way back through the brush.

She was there to greet us.

"It's pretty isn't it?" She asked with a grin.

"It sure is. It's so peaceful." Ronnie Said. "And it glows!"

"This Stream was a big reason why my husband and I bought this house. It was the icing on the cake when we were looking at farm properties. Something just told us to buy it."

"What's down the tunnel?" I asked curiously.

"Oh I don't know." She stared through the brush. "My son claimed he went down there once... but didn't really give any details."

Ronnie glanced at me with confusion as it was the first time he had heard of her son.

"Mrs. Blank, if you don't mind, can you point out where your husband's accident happened so we can get the proper shot?" I asked.

"Sure," she replied faintly as if I was waking her out of a daydream.

We walked over to one of the barns.

"It happened right here in front of this barn." She pointed with her cane. "It was a Tuesday afternoon in the heat of early August...His intention was to cut through all this brush, so we could enjoy the stream more." She sighed then started to walk toward the house.

After walking about 10 or 15 feet she turned around. "I'll meet you boys back inside in a few minutes. I would like to get this interview done."

I nodded my head.

CHAPTER 8

The Interview

I mic'd up Mrs. Blank and did a quick sound check. Ronnie hit record...

ME: Mrs. Blank, many people have alluded to you studying Wicca and being a witch. Is it true?"

She had a big smile on her face.

MRS. BLANK: No, it is not true.

ME: So where did and does everyone get this idea from?

MRS. BLANK: When my son was younger, he was playing out back with a friend one day. Wanting to show off, my son brought his friend to the stream and tunnel.

She paused briefly and shook her head.

MRS. BLANK: I remember it like it was yesterday. My son's friend claims he saw something...apparently some sort of owl. He claims the owl whispered to him that the witch was near and he should run for his life.

I was thinking about Ronnie claiming to hear an owl earlier, but I did not glance over to him as Mrs. Blank was still giving a sound bite. She continued...

MRS. BLANK: Startled, the kid fell down and scraped up his

body. My son followed and they both ran back through the brush, which caused more wounds and tears on their clothes from the prickers. When they got back to the house, I began to clean their wounds when my cat at the time walked into the room. She was a black cat with green eyes. Her name was Nicki. She was a good little kitty. Anyway, my son's friend was spooked by the cat and claims it whispered the same thing the owl did. He was frightened and ran home. The next day his mother called me and said that her son can no longer hang out here. After this incident, everything became different in town. My assumption is that this woman told others, and I'm assuming it spread as a rumor.

ME: So you think the mother believed her son?

MRS. BLANK: Yes I do. Not to mention. I have an aunt who does follow the Wiccan religion. I later found out that my son had mentioned that to his friend. Again, being at the age where a kid wants to show off and gain attention.

Mrs. Blank started to tear up.

MRS. BLANK: I'm sure between the incident I told you, my auntie the witch, me walking with a cane, this big ol' spooky house, and us raising and butchering our own meat...it contributes to the rumor. And it only got worse in the late 90's when that popular witch movie came out. I don't remember the name of it...

ME: The Blair Witch Project?

MRS. BLANK: Yes, yes, that's it. Well, the rumor spread like wildfire. I have been the 'Witch of Elberton' for over ten years now. Do you know what it's like to be falsely branded as something you're not? Oh, it's horrible. I don't wish it on anyone."

She paused to wipe the tears from her face with a tissue.

MRS. BLANK: In that time, I haven't been able to keep any friends and my son was deeply affected by it. Especially when he got to high school.

I couldn't help but feel horrible for this woman. I could see now why she wanted her story told so badly.

ME: I'm very sorry to hear all of this Mrs. Blank.

MRS. BLANK: And then...when the Damien incident happened...the Inquirer twisted the story and made me a witch in their headlines. Do you know how much this effects my life? They took a rumor from a little town in Georgia and made it national! Those bastards. So mean and heartless they are. I even heard that one of those late night talk show hosts made a joke about it.

I shook my head with sorrow.

ME: No, I can't even imagine. This is a very unfortunate situation.

How come you haven't moved?

MRS. BLANK: I tried. After my husband died I looked for new houses for me and my son. Every time I found something it fell through. Then, after my son died, I looked again. Nothing. Every time, it falls through. It's like I am stuck at this house, on this property, with that stream behind me, in this town that believes I'm a witch! And now that I made headlines in a national magazine...who would even rent to me? Maybe I'm cursed? Who knows...

She chuckled with tears running down her face. I almost felt like I didn't want to continue. I thought of Dr. Hickenbottom and everything he said. He told me to accept what was ahead and that I had free will. I knew we had plenty for my final project. I flirted with the idea of stopping, but on the story side of things, I knew there was so much more I had to ask. What about this owl? Was it real? Was it the same one Ronnie heard? Her pain was deep and it was all coming out on camera. It made me uncomfortable, but I knew it was good material. I had to keep going....

ME: We interviewed the police officer that came to your house when you called after Damien returned. He said he found a big golden nugget in the back of your yard. Do you know where that came from?

MRS. BLANK: One day my husband found nuggets of gold inside the stream tunnel. He came back delighted. You should have seen him! He actually grabbed me and started dancing with me in the kitchen. He thought we were rich!. A few days later, he brought back about five pieces and said there was a ton more. But when he went back the next day, he claimed they were gone. When Officer Ritter found a nugget the other week, I just assumed there was one out back that was left over. I figured it would help with finding the truth of everything, so I let him take it as evidence. He was passionate about finding answers. After going through everything that I've been through, I want answers too! I deserve to know!

ME: Understandable. How did Mr. Blank die?

MRS. BLANK: My husband and I had planned to rid ourselves of the brush out back. As you see, I walk with a cane, so I can't go through that brush and I wanted to enjoy the sight and sounds of the stream too. It was a Saturday... he went to the barn and revved up the chainsaw. My son was outside cutting the lawn at the time and I was in the kitchen preparing food. Between the lawn mower and the chainsaw, there was a lot of noise out back. It couldn't have been more than five Minutes that the chainsaw was on before I heard a scream that still sends chills down my spine to this day.

She paused, again wiping tears from her eyes.

MRS. BLANK: I ran out back and my....my.... My husband's head was lying about 10 feet away from his body and my son was standing over his father's head. There was blood everywhere. I told my son to run in the house and call 911. I didn't want him to witness this...this...this atrocity anymore. You know?"

She then started hyperventilating as the tears flowed. Ronnie and I stopped the tape to calm her down. I got her a glass of water as Ronnie put his arm on her shoulder and comforted her as best he could. After about 10 minutes went by, she agreed to continue.

ME: Mrs. Blank, what did the authorities say about your husband's accident?

MRS. BLANK: They said it was a chainsaw accident. That he lost control of it and accidentally decapitated himself.

I was getting more and more confident as a journalist.

ME: What do you believe?

She stared at me with the coldest look I have ever seen in my life.

MRS. BLANK: I believe... that something cut his head off.

ME: Like what?

MRS. BLANK: I wish I knew, Mark. I really do. When my son ran and got to his father's head...he claimed that his father whispered one last thing to him.

She paused.

MRS. BLANK: He claims his father told him to stay away from the tunnel.

ME: Why do you think? What's dangerous about that tunnel?

MRS. BLANK: I don't know. I'm not able to even get through the brush with my leg. You know...it's obvious that my husband and son knew things that I didn't. They probably kept things from me so I wouldn't freak out about them.

ME: Mrs. Blank, let's talk about your son. How was he affected by this horrible accident?

MRS. BLANK: He was devastated. He was only 16 or 17 when it happened. He had his senior prom and graduation coming and skipped both. Not to mention he had just gotten his driver's license and was going through that teenager-to-man transition. He couldn't wait to get out of high school because for so long he was labeled the son of a witch. Certainly, this incident didn't help the rumor. You can hear it now right? 'Man's head cut off at the witch's house.' My son didn't deserve this. He didn't.

She shook her head with tears in her eyes.

MRS. BLANK: He went to community college the following fall but he wanted out really bad. He wanted to move away to a school where no one would know him. I used a few golden nuggets that my husband had stored and that helped pay the way so he could go to college in Florida. He would come home during the holidays and the summers to stay with me. I started to notice changes in him. He became moody and manic. Come to find out he was addicted to prescription pills. He would mix them with alcohol often too. He even use to sniff Oxycodone. Every time I tried to get him help he would resist. He was in denial. He used to sit on the back porch with a gun in the summer. When I would ask what he was doing, he claimed he was waiting for the owl, and that when it appeared... he would kill it. There were many nights where I would cry myself to sleep. I was so concerned that he would be taken from me next. He was out of control.

ME: How did he die Mrs. Blank?

MRS. BLANK: One day, he got really drunk. Instead of sitting on the porch with the gun, he decided to go to the stream. I remember hearing him cursing real loud as he walked toward it. I was looking out the window upstairs. He was very emotional and was saying things like 'I'm coming to get you', and 'There is no escaping your karma'. I couldn't stop him. All I could do was hope he came back. But...he never came back.

She stopped and stared at the ground.

MRS. BLANK: Two hours had gone by...so I called the police. They found him lying dead next to the stream from a self-inflicted gun wound. The autopsy stated that he was very drunk and high on pills. I can't help but think of my husband's last message to his son. And 4 or 5 years later he goes to the tunnel and ends up dead...

She looked up from the floor and stared directly in my eyes. She had sweltering big bags under her eyes and her cheeks were reddish. She appeared to be worn down from the trauma and exhausted from this interview. I stared back at her.

ME: We're almost there Mrs. Blank. Hold tight. I gotta ask, what do you make of this owl? Have you ever seen or heard it during the day time?

MRS BLANK: I do hear it during the day every now and again, yes, but I have only seen it once. It was the other day actually. I had just let Damien out on his leash and was in the kitchen. I glanced out the window and saw the owl on top of one of the rabbit hutches. The rabbits were going crazy. You could hear them scattering in fear. But the owl just stared at me, making that awful hooting noise.

ME: How long did this stare down take place?

MRS. BLANK: Oh I would say 30 Seconds, maybe less. It wasn't long, but it felt long. I became angry. I bolted around the corner as fast as I could with my cane and went out the back door. But the owl was gone.

ME: Why did you feel angry?"

MRS. BLANK: I guess...I felt as though it took my family. I felt angry enough to confront it and maybe smack it with my cane. I don't know...

She sighed.

MRS. BLANK: And go figure...the next day is when Damien went missing...

ME: Can you tell me about that day? And the incident as a whole?

MRS. BLANK: Sure. My morning routine is I let Damien out on his leash when I'm making the coffee in the morning. Everything went as normal. When I went to bring him in about 15 Minutes later he was gone. Almost as though someone unhooked him off his leash and just took him. I didn't hear any barking, whining, noises...nothing at all. He just vanished. I was devastated. He's my only friend.... Anyway, about four days later he showed back up, on his leash right at the back door. He was very excited to see me.

She smiled as she relived the moment.

MRS. BLANK: But then I notice something. There was no noise coming out of him. It was so weird. So strange. I took him outside to play and held his favorite toy as high as I could. This usually provokes him to bark. Well, everything went as normal...except there was no noise coming out when he barked. I felt like I was in some sort of movie or something. Like it was a scene and it was in slow motion with no sound. I felt myself get nauseous and dizzy. When I calmed myself down a tad, I called the police. What else could I do? What would anyone do? That's when Officer Ritter came out. He of course was in awe too. I can't imagine what the police department thinks of me.

She cracked a sad grin. She sarcastically finished her thought in the third person.

MRS. BLANK: The witch's house...where her husband gets decapitated, son commits suicide, dog goes mute. They've had some strange calls to this house. That's for sure.

ME: Okay Mrs. Blank. I think we're done.

She jumped in.

MRS. BLANK: Wait. There's one more question, Mark!

She looked intense.

MRS. BLANK: What do I make of this stream and tunnel?!

She became very animated and passionate. Her voice raised.

MRS. BLANK: Yeah, you know I think...I think that as beautiful as it sounds and looks...it's evil personified. I've never been inside that tunnel. But my husband and son have. And we know what happened to them. Don't go in there boys. Don't do it!

CHAPTER 9

The Ending

After packing the car with our gear, Ronnie started her up and drove up the dirt road as we started our journey back to campus. It didn't take long before Ronnie broke the silence with a bang.

"Holy shit balls bro!!!!! Wooooooooooooo, can you believe what just happened!?"

I was smiling hard.

"Bro, you were amazing in there! You were like fucking….fucking...Barbara Walters out that bitch! You got a future Mr. Calloway! Wow bro! Wow!"

"Thanks...I'm exhausted though," I replied.

"Shit...I'm tired from just listening to you guys. It was an emotional rollercoaster bro. The crying, the drama, the pain. Can you imagine how this is going evoke emotion in the viewer?"

"Yeah man." I replied softly. Talking more just seemed to suck more energy from me. I felt like I just played 5 straight games of basketball with a short and fast point guard that I had to cover. I closed my eyes and listened to Ronnie's excitement.

"You got gold bro! No pun intended," he chuckled. "The only thing is...there are so many unanswered questions. Where did the gold come from? Why did Officer Ritter really get canned? How did Mrs. Blank's husband and son really die? What's this owl all about? And the big one…What's in that tunnel? Where does the stream lead to? Some lake or pond or something?" Ronnie paused….after about 30 seconds of silence, a light bulb seemed to go off in his head. "Bro, this isn't over is it?"

"Not at all." I said, still with my eyes closed and laid back in the passenger seat.

"Soooooooo...what's the next move then?"

"I have to find an expert of some kind so we can get answers." I said.

"Aaahhhh that makes sense. Some sort of like...paranormal buff right? Hmmmm. I think I know of one bro. This guy that writes for TRUTHISSCARY.com. He talks about all sorts of topics. He's an author too. His name is Virgil something or other. He was actually in my dream, the one I told you I had when I suggested the Elberton story. Maybe this is supposed to happen."

"Well." I said. "We can add him to the list of candidates. I'm gonna have to find the right person for the job. But this project is left with so many unanswered questions. I can see it driving the audience nuts if I only used what was recorded so far."

"How much time do you have before you have to hand it in for class?" He asked.

"I got about two weeks." I opened my eyes and sat up as I started to come to life a little more just thinking of the work ahead of me. "I'm gonna have to put this documentary together with what I have now. I can hand it in for class and just get that out of the way. Then I can send the potential expert a copy of the project. This will give them a good sense of what's happening. Almost like a demo tape. When they come on board to finish the film, I can get them to Mrs. Blank's house and we can shoot their investigations. Then we sit them down for an interview. When that's done, I can take that footage and add it to the film, creating an ending. Hopefully with answers."

Ronnie was smiling from ear to ear. "You're a genius, bro! That's a great idea! It makes sense because you don't need the expert's sound bites throughout. The expert is the ending!"

"Correct," I said confidently, "This will give the audience the anticipation to see the dramatic conclusion that we ourselves, are witnessing at the present time. The footage of the expert will be the frosting on the cake. The conclusion. Act three."

Ronnie grinned. "Wait now...is that a fucking Vegan cake bro?"

I laughed. "Yeah man...It's rabbit free."

We both burst out laughing.

CHAPTER 10

The Playback

Knowing that I had a long two weeks ahead of me, it was important to get a good night's rest. My intention was to take the mini DV tapes to the editing lab after classes and start working on the documentary. I couldn't help but wonder how certain sound bites would look next to each other and how the story would unfold on screen. After breakfast, I knocked on Ronnie's door to get the last tape from Mrs. Blank's house. Ronnie opened the door and weed smoke came pouring out.

"Bro, it's been two days, I gotta catch up on my Zen," he said with a grin.

I chuckled. "Can I get the last tape please? I'm gonna start editing after classes today after I bring back the equipment."

"Sure,"he said. He walked to his desk, then handed the tape to me. "Hold on Mark. How much time to do you have before your first class? Do you have a few? I mean...I can't stop thinking about the stream and the tunnel. Let's take a second look on the tape."

I paused and thought about it. "Alright, I can spare about 10 minutes."

I went and got the camera, popped the tape in and put it on review mode. I hit rewind as we watched the Mrs. Blank interview in rewind patiently waiting for the B-roll footage of the stream to appear. Once the stream footage appeared I pressed play on the tape as we watched on the little flip screen attached to the camera.

"Wow bro." Ronnie blurted. "It's so damn beautiful. Do you see that goldish glow that's coming out of the tunnel?"

"Yeah it is kind of goldish isn't it?" I asked as I squinted intensely.

"Holy shit balls!" Ronnie yelled. "Do you….."

"Yes."

I cut him off.

"I see it." I hit pause on the footage and pressed my head against Ronnie's wall. All I could do was smirk and shake my head.

"Bring it back." Ronnie said. "Bring that back please bro! Tell me I didn't see what you saw!?"

I rewound the footage a few seconds and pressed play...and there it was again. Just for about ten seconds as Ronnie scanned the top of the tunnel with the camera, we saw the owl stare at us with reddish beady eyes. Chills ran through my body.

"Wow. I feel like that mother fucker is wondering who the hell these two young dudes are and why they're here." Ronnie said passionately.

"So I guess you did hear an owl as you were approaching the brush huh?"

"Yep. I guess I'm not nuts bro," he replied.

"Alright man, I gotta get going to class."

The most tedious part of any video project is digitizing, also known as capturing. It's the process of transferring the footage on tape and storing it onto a hard drive. It can and will drive any editor nutty because you have to capture in real time. So if you're digitizing a 30 minute clip, it will take 30 minutes to do so. It also sucks up gigabytes, which is why I bought my own terabyte hard drive to capture on. There was no way I'm leaving this important footage on the school's hard drive.

There were 2 other students in the editing lab working on their own projects. One kid was from my class. I glanced over to the IMac station that he was at. The clip he was editing was of an older guy with grey hair in a military uniform. He looked over and we made eye contact. He recognized me.

"Hey man, how's your project coming out?" He asked.

"Good," I said, "I'm actually digitizing now. My shoots ran long."

"Cool. I'm just finishing up now. Just reviewing it making sure it's good to present to Hickenbottom and the class."

"What did you do it on?" I asked.

"Oh I did it on my grandfather who was a navy lieutenant," he said proudly. "What did you do yours on?"

I didn't really know what to say. "Uhhhhh....well...I did mine on a witch who supposedly made her dog not bark anymore."

I was just trying to get out of the conversation as I felt uncomfortable.

All of a sudden the kid next to us jumped in.

"Hey man, are you talking about the witch from Elberton?

"Yeah," I replied.

"No shit. My big cousin was the officer on that case," he said.

"Really? Officer Ritter?"

"Yeah, he was fired because of that crazy witch bitch."

"Wait, what? I interviewed him and he didn't say that." I was in shock.

"I don't know when you spoke to him, but I just spoke to him yesterday. That's what he found out recently. She put in a complaint that he was stealing and a few attorneys came into the police station and said my cousin needed to be let go or they would sue."

"I interviewed her yesterday and she...She said she wanted him to find answers. She seemed fond of him."

"Maybe that bitch is bipolar or something man. Fuck her!" He said passionately.

The other kid chimed in with a smile. "Sounds like you got yourself a controversial topic my friend."

"Yeah I guess I do," I replied with a forced grin.

I got up and went to the hallway so I could call Ronnie.

"That's crazy bro!?" Ronnie said through the phone, "I can't say that I believe it though. Mrs. Blank just doesn't seem like the type to get attorneys involved. Dude, she just wanted answers, we saw the pain. It was authentic."

"I know," I replied, "But we don't know what we're dealing with here. Maybe she is a witch. Maybe that's her gold and she doesn't want anyone taking it. Maybe she's deceiving us?"

"Right," Ronnie said sarcastically, "And she did an imaginary surgery on her dog? With no incision?"

"Good point," I replied.

"Listen, I was going to wait till you got back to the apartment...but since I got you on the horn...."

"What?" I said expecting some sort of more strange news.

"Bro, the RA came to the room and said they needed to speak to me downstairs. When I got down there it was the RA and the some other guy I've never seen before. He said that he knows I've been smoking marijuana in the apartment and if they catch me with it on me in any capacity I would be expelled from housing and maybe the college as a whole."

"Oh wow." I said.

"Yeah, but I don't get it. I'm cool with the RA…. shit...I've even smoked with that motherfucker before! Why would the RA rat me out? And you know damn well the smell doesn't creep into the hallway. We've tested it before. It doesn't make sense."

"Who was this guy? What was his title?" I asked.

"He said he worked in a special drug unit for the state university police. He had on a black suit. He looked like he was straight out of the Matrix! Like fucking Agent Smith and shit! I felt like it was a threat of some sort."

"What do you mean?"

"Like he was using the weed as leverage."

"Leverage for what?" I felt anxiety as the conversation continued.

"Like...like chill out on the Mrs. Blank stuff or else..." He replied as his voice shook.

"Ronnie, you smoke a lot. Maybe you just got caught. Don't bug out dude. Just quit for a little bit. Okay? I don't need a new roommate any time soon." I said.

"Yeah," he replied, "I'll try to chill out for now. Just keep your eyes peeled. I have a strange feeling."

We hung up and I went back into the editing lab.

Officer Ritter's little cousin was still there. After I sat down, he tapped me on my shoulder. "Hey man, I hope you don't mind...I was watching your footage as it was digitizing. It's pretty damn captivating. But...I have to ask you...Did you notice that owl in the tunnel?"

"Yeah," I took a deep breath, "I saw it."

CHAPTER 11

The Final Cut

Three long days went by and I had finished the documentary. Well, the school version anyway. I was exhausted after having spent at least 6 hours per day in the editing lab. I knew I had something special because other students would stop and stare, or ask questions about what I was working on. I had their attention. Mentally, I was just tapped out. Watching the Mrs. Blank sound bites again and again was heart-wrenching. Playing with the slow motion features on the owl in the tunnel footage gave me anxiety every single time I worked on it. Summer break often invaded my thoughts and I wanted this to be over.

Not wanting to rely on anyone, I decided to use my own voice as the narrator so I could easily edit in the true ending when it was time. I added plenty of motion control shots of still newspaper and magazine clippings. The shots give the film a "national story" feel to it. I named the documentary, "The Elberton Enigma." I felt that the word "enigma" nicely wrapped up this mysterious story of a widowed woman who was labeled the town witch. She was an enigma. The dog's strange surgery was an enigma. The owl was an enigma. The gold...the tunnel...the deaths...Enigma just seemed like the perfect word. Go figure the town started with an "E", so it just sounded and felt right to me.

The Elberton Enigma came out to 37 Minutes. I just felt it was too deep of a story to only do the 15 Minutes that Dr. Hickenbottom assigned. My next task would be getting approval from him to hand in a documentary that was double what he asked because 37 Minutes seemed perfect to me. I figured the new ending with the expert footage would end up being around 20 Minutes, and that would give me a solid 1 hour completed project. I had hope that this could work out just perfect. I burned 5 DVD's. One for me, Ronnie, Mrs. Blank, Dr. Hickenbottom, and whoever our "expert" candidate was going to be. I sent Ronnie a text message to let him know I'm coming home with it.

When I got there, I walked in and smelt an aroma. But for once it wasn't weed! It was popcorn!

"Hey bro," Ronnie said with excitement, "I'm so ready to watch this. I made plenty of popcorn. Of course butter-free for the world's best Vegan filmmaker."

I laughed. "Thanks man. Here's your very own DVD copy. Pop it in."

"With pleasure!" He said with much enthusiasm.

The documentary ended in a dramatic fashion…

Creepy music fades up...

NARRATOR: Through all the speculation...We still don't know what the stream means, and what's in this mysterious tunnel. (B-roll footage of the stream and tunnel)

MRS. BLANK: "I think...I think that as beautiful as it sounds and looks...it's evil personified. We know there is gold somewhere and we know there is an owl.

NARRATOR: A strange owl that looks over the tunnel? A nocturnal bird which shows up during the day. What does it all mean?

MRS. BLANK: The nearest I can tell...The owl is like...the protector maybe? Yeah, the eyes and ears. I've never been inside that tunnel, but my husband and son have. And we know what happened to them…

NARRATOR: There is but only one way to solve this enigma...and that is...to enter…the tunnel.

MRS. BLANK: Don't go in that tunnel. Don't do it boys! It's not worth it. (B-roll footage of the owl spotted in the tunnel in slow motion.)

And the documentary ends with the owl footage on pause for 5 or so seconds and the creepy music ends. Roll credits.

"Fucking holy shit balls bro! My skin is crawling right now!" Ronnie yelled.

I smiled and replied, "Glad you liked."

He continued, "This is amazing Mark! The Elberton Enigma is going to evoke many emotions in people and it is completely different than other documentaries that I have seen. Bro, once we get the expert in and get some answers, it's going to be ready for Netflix...maybe even a movie theater!"

"We need the right expert to come in and end it off with a bang." I replied.

"Bro, I have a good feeling about this Virgil guy. I did some research on him and emailed you some of his articles so you can read. He covers all sorts of paranormal shit. Ghosts, UFO's, Bigfoot, vampires etc. He may love this lead. When he sees the Elberton Enigma, he's gonna be all over it. I guarantee it. I mean, if nothing else, he can at least give the film coverage on his website."

"Cool." I said. "I'll read up on him tomorrow. For now, I need some rest because I have to talk to my professor first thing in the morning before my class starts. I want to make sure he will accept a 37 minute project."

"Bro, do you get to play this for the class?" Ronnie asked.

I nodded my head yes.

"Oh man, I want to be there for that."

"I'll get permission for a guest when I talk to him then."

The next day I had beat Dr. Hickenbottom to the classroom. I was sitting outside the door when he arrived. He looked shocked to see me.

"Young Mr. Callaway. What brings you in early?" He said.

"Well, my project came out to 37 Minutes and I wanted to make sure you would still accept it for a grade."

He raised his eyebrows. "That's a pretty long project. How come you didn't just edit it down to 15 minutes? One of the keys in this business is following directions."

"I know." I replied with a look of concern. "But I have a desire to shoot more and make this a feature film to pitch to a production company or maybe Netflix directly. So doing it at 15 minutes would have been more work for me. Dr. Hickenbottom, I would really appreciate it if you would accept it."

He paused. "That's very ambitious of you. Okay, I will take it for a grade. However, I cannot enter it into the film student festival for next semester."

I smiled. "I understand. Will I still be able to have the class view it though?"

"Yes, sure. I don't see why not. You're proud of it I see."

"Yes sir I am. It was a ton of work and took a lot of emotion." I replied.

"Okay. I will take it. How deep did you go?"

"We went pretty deep." I said with excitement.

"We?"

"Oh, yes, my roommate Ronnie did the camera for me. Is it okay if he comes to the class when we view it?"

"Certainly. Not a problem at all."

I was thrilled that Dr. Hickenbottom was going to accept it for my final. I text messaged Ronnie to let him know, and also informed him of the time and date it would be viewed in class. While I was waiting for class to begin, I looked through my email and read the articles Ronnie sent me about Virgil Riley. Ronnie was right, this guy did seem as though he was an expert in many paranormal topics. He seemed like the perfect guy for the job. I found his direct email on his website and started typing a message to him.

Mr. Riley,

My name is Mark Calloway and I am a student at Ashford University in Marietta Georgia. I recently did a documentary on the 'Witch of Elberton' after her dog showed up with no more barking abilities. I interviewed Mrs. Blank, the officer on the case and more.

Needless to say, this story snowballed into many mysteries that I cannot explain. I am currently looking to bring on an "expert" to investigate and make sense of these mysteries on camera. You seem like a good candidate to be a part of this special project.

I will mail you a copy of the unfinished documentary entitled, "The

Elberton Enigma" for your review. I hope you will consider this opportunity.

Sincerely,

Mark Calloway

I wrote down his business mailing address in North Carolina and put it in my pocket. Later on, I'll have Ronnie take me to the post office to send the DVD out. We'll see what happens. I felt accomplished...and the day just started.

CHAPTER 12

The Premiere

About halfway through the screening of the "Elberton Enigma" a girl in my class got up and walked out. Ronnie leaned over and whispered to me, "Bro, she looked like she was going to puke." My eyes scanned the room trying to see people's reactions as best I could in the dimly-lit room. One kid looked like he was on a rollercoaster that was slowly creeping up to the high peak, only to drop down at any second. Another kid I saw with his head down on his desk as though he was sleeping. A girl sitting parallel to us was glued to the screen with her mouth wide open and eyebrows slightly raised. My mind couldn't help but wonder what my classmates were thinking at that very moment. The end was approaching. Ronnie and I made eye contact. He shook his head knowing that the dramatic ending was coming, and our infamous owl would be making its big appearance in front of a live audience. Here it comes….

Everyone in the room gasped as they saw the owl for the first time. Dr. Hickenbottom himself nearly jumped out of his seat as Mrs. Blank's powerful statement blared over the slow motion of the owl. The screen faded to black and the room started to clap. Boy did it feel good. Ronnie was super excited as he jolted my shoulder as the lights came on.

"Very well done. That was over the top, Mr. Callaway," Dr.

Hickebottom said from the front of the class. "The owl at the end reminded me of when we first saw Jaws, and Brody claimed they needed a bigger boat." He shook his head in amazement.

"Wow, that's a great compliment!" I replied with much pride. Jaws was one of, if not the best thriller and horror movies ever.

Dr. Hickenbottom continued speaking to the class. "Now, Mr. Calloway informed me last week that he would be completing this documentary and attempting to package and distribute it to the public. I think you got a heck of a shot, Mark. This was a riveting piece of work!"

"Aren't you scared?" A girl from class spoke out concerned, "I mean, you discovered a mystery that is completely unsolved, and you wanna dig up more? Aren't you freaked out?"

I smiled. "Yeah, I'm creeped out...But I feel the need to finish what I started. I think fear is part of being an investigative filmmaker and journalist. You know...not knowing what can pop up next. The unknown can be scary. This whole experience so far has been one surprise after another, but I'm motivated to make documentaries as my career. That's really what's keeping me going." The class seemed to respect my answer as I spoke with conviction.

Ironically, Ronnie and I sat at the same table in the cafeteria where he brought up the idea of covering the 'Witch of Elberton' story.

"Bro..." He said with a straight face. "You got yourself a winner. Those students felt that emotion. Your professor felt that emotion. I mean...One girl left the room!" He said passionately.

"I know. How about the 'Jaws' comparison?!" I said with overwhelming excitement. "That was like... the ultimate horror thriller. People wouldn't even go in the water for like 10 years man."

"Exactly!" Ronnie fired back, "All you're missing is your dramatic ending. This story unfolds similar to 'Jaws' in the sense of you not seeing the shark till later in the movie, but you knew it was there the whole time. But once you saw the shark, then it became a battle to the death. Who was going to live? The shark or the people on the boat?!"

I paused and thought about what Ronnie had just said.

"Dude, you just sent chills down my spine with that comment." Ronnie anticipated for me to continue.

"If 'Jaws' is the owl, and we just discovered it...then that means it's time for our battle to the death right?"

Ronnie's eyebrows raised. "Yeah, I suppose. We're the ones on the boat in the middle of the ocean right?" I nodded my head as he paused.

"Well, we don't have to go back out in the ocean if you don't want to bro. We can sit comfortably knowing it's one hell of a 37 Minute Documentary."

"No." I replied. "Too many questions with no answers. We have to go back out in the ocean to make sure…" Ronnie Jumped in.

"Hey, speaking of going back. Did you hear from Virgil yet? It's been a week or so right?"

"I haven't heard back from him." I took out my phone to check my email.

Go figure I had an email waiting for me! I started to read out loud to Ronnie.

Mark,

I viewed the DVD. Well done. Please give me a call ASAP. We should talk.

My Cell Phone is 336-xxx-xxxx

Regards,

Virgil

Ronnie got excited. "Bro, you should call now! I'm curious, aren't you?"

"For sure. Keep the table. I'm gonna to step outside and ring him."

The phone rang only twice before a deep raspy voice answered.

"Hello this is Virgil."

"Hey Virgil, this is Mark Calloway. I just got your email."

"Hi Mark." He did not participate in any small talk. He just jumped right in.

"What was your feeling when you first saw the owl?"

"Well, we didn't see the owl until we reviewed the tapes. But when I did see it, it was kind of freaky."

"Mark..." He paused. "Have you ever heard of the Georgia Guidestones?"

"No, I have not," I replied.

"Okay, well they are one of, if not the strangest United States mysteries." He paused again... "They are located in Elberton Georgia Mark."

"Really?" I said in shock. "What are these...guidestones all about?"

"I'm going to let you do your own research on that. I could talk about them for days."

"And you think they could be linked to the owl?" I asked as anxiety filled my body.

"Very well could be," he paused again, "I would like to take you up on your offer and be a part of this documentary. Would you be able to pay for my travel and hotel?

"Okay, yeah let's do it." I replied as I was happy to know he would not charge us.

"Yes, we will cover your costs no problem."

He continued talking with his raspy voice. "Good. I figure we can get everything done in two or three days. We need to go to the stones, I need to talk to Barbara Blank, and most importantly...I need to get in that tunnel."

I felt like I wanted to throw up. The thought of going in that tunnel, the thought of the owl, the thought of some strange United States mystery that I had never heard of.

Virgil went on. "As soon as you coordinate everything with Mrs. Blank, email me the details and I will arrive on the start date. I just need a few weeks to take care of some things."

"He's in." I told Ronnie as I sat back down at our table.

"Really? That's great bro! Did he mention any of his thoughts on the owl or Mrs. Blank?"

"No...He was very short-winded and to the point." I stared down at the table as I felt myself kind of drift into a blur.

"Mark, are you okay?" Ronnie asked concerned.

I paused, then looked back up at Ronnie. "He informed me that the Georgia Guidestones are in Elberton and there could be a correlation."

Ronnie squinted his face up. "Georgia what??? What's that?"

"I asked the same thing. He told me to look them up."

Ronnie took out his phone and googled it. "Holy shit balls bro....look at these things!" He showed me his phone. They were huge stones...about 20 feet high. A message consisting of a set of

10 guidelines was engraved.

"I can't believe this was right under our noses the whole time bro." Ronnie said as he took his phone back. I felt like I was going to throw up again as Ronnie started to read the guidelines out loud.

Maintain humanity under 500,000,000 in perpetual balance with nature.

Guide reproduction wisely — improving fitness and diversity.

Unite humanity with a living new language.

Rule passion — faith — tradition — and all things with tempered reason.

Protect people and nations with fair laws and just courts.

Let all nations rule internally resolving external disputes in a world court.

Avoid petty laws and useless officials.

Balance personal rights with social duties.

Prize truth — beauty — love — seeking harmony with the infinite.

Be not a cancer on the earth — Leave room for nature — Leave room for nature.

Ronnie continued. "Bro, if that isn't enough...these 10 guidelines are written in 8 different languages! English, Spanish, Swahili, Hindi, Hebrew, Arabic, Chinese and Russian. Oh and around the edges of the square are written the names of 4 ancient languages, one per edge. They're Babylonian, Greek, Sanskrit and Ancient Egyptian. Bro, we're in fucking Georgia...who reads ancient languages? Forget ancient...who reads even Chinese or Arabic out here? This is a global monument with a global message Mark."

I looked at Ronnie and shook my head.

"What the hell could be the correlation Virgil is referring to?"

"I don't know." Ronnie said. "But...There is an inscription that says 'Let these be guidestones to an Age of Reason'. Bro, do you know how many people would have to die to get down to 500 Million? How many people are there on earth? Like 7 billion? What the fuck bro! What else did Virgil say man?!"

I looked back down at the table. "Well...He said we need to go to the stones, that he needs to talk to Mrs. Blank, and he needs to go into the tunnel."

Ronnie's face dropped.

"Well...alright then... so Virgil is your Quint... We're gonna need a bigger boat...and I'm gonna need to start smoking weed again!"

As frightened as I was...He made me chuckle.

CHAPTER 13

The Expert

Ronnie and I pulled up to the Days Inn in Elberton. Everything was arranged. We were to meet Virgil, then head over to the Guidestones. The next day we were to go to Mrs. Blank's for lunch and capture all the footage needed. Day 3 was reserved for any odds and ends we may need to wrap up. Ronnie was nice enough to put up the money for Virgil's accommodations. We worked out a deal where Ronnie would get 15% of the proceeds of the final project. I thought it was fair, as not only did he pay for Virgil and all the trips to Elberton, but he was donating his time. We were both confident that this project would become a worldwide phenomenon.

As we parked, I saw a bald headed man wave to us. I got out of the car and walked over to him assuming it was Virgil.

"Virgil?" I asked?

"Yes, you must be Mark." He reached out his hand to shake as Ronnie followed suit.

Virgil stood around 5'8" and looked to be in his early 50's. His bald head combined with his raspy deep voice seemed to give him the aura of an authority figure.

"I have an idea guys...After we get everything into the rooms, why don't we go get some lunch and get to know each other. Then we can head over to the Guidestones," I said enthusiastically.

"Sounds good to me," Virgil replied.

Ronnie nudged me in the arm. "Hey bro, let's go to the spot where we interviewed the girl about Mrs. Blank. I think she liked you. Let her know you're in town...if you know what I'm saying." He smiled.

"Yeah, yeah, yeah. Sure, we can go there," I replied. And immediately visions of Victoria popped into my head.

The three of us sat down in our booth and started to skim through the menu. I scanned the restaurant looking for Victoria, but did not see her pretty face anywhere.

"So Virgil, tell us about your background and how did you make it to TRUTHISSCARY.COM?" I asked.

"Well, it was in the 70's that I woke up. I became a truth seeker and I realized that I was not me. And that my spirit was separated from my mind and body. I learned meditation and started tapping into our true source. Besides the spiritual side, I started doing a ton of research on various alternative topics and I was captivated on my findings. I started with JFK, then went on to the Vatican, and then moved on to Roswell and so forth. I realized that the government is not who is truly in control."

Ronnie interrupted, "Illuminati?"

"Yeah...Well that's one word for it," Virgil continued. "That's a buzzword that gets a lot of hits on the internet these days. It doesn't matter what we call it. The bottom line is the government, and all governments have to answer to someone." He paused. "Anyway, I started a newsletter putting this information out in the 90's. When the internet exploded I started writing for alternative topic websites. After 9/11 happened, things changed. Alternative topics become more popular and people started waking up a little bit. Documentaries on this stuff started coming out and what not. I helped produce a few actually. In the late 2000's, TIS asked me to come on board to be a full time reporter. And here I am."

"So you dedicated your life to conspiracies?" Ronnie asked.

"To truth." Virgil said, "To find the truth at all costs...even if your life must be taken for it."

"So...You're willing to die for truth?" Ronnie asked.

"Yes." Virgil spoke with passion. "So wasn't Gandhi, Dr. King and many others. Even the Buddha, who ate a meal that he knew was spoiled because he didn't want to refuse it from the person that offered it to him. It was a gift that he gladly accepted. I think everyone is willing to die when they reach the point of finding their soul and have a self-realization."

"Are you married? Any kids?" Ronnie continued to ask questions.

"No. I stopped caring about marriage in the 80's. It just isn't for me." He said.

"That's interesting. How come?" I asked.

"Well." Virgil smirked as he began to speak again. "The ego is what wants to be attached to another person. The ego loves affection and the ego loves to know that someone cares about them. However, when you are spiritually free and in complete love with everyone and everything, you do not need the attachment of a spouse. Being single is freedom. Marriage usually ends in divorce or unhappiness because the two people rely so heavily on each other for happiness. But one must be happy with themselves first. And that...is not easy to find my friends. I have not crossed paths with a woman that is spiritually awakened yet. So that tells me the universe doesn't want marriage for me. So I stay single and keep my focus to my work. Not only my research on truth, but my own spiritual development."

"Freedom." Ronnie shook his head. "So...no calling the wife to tell her where you are or where you're going. And no burden of having to spend time with her? I dig that bro!"

Virgil chuckled. "Relationships seem to be conflict and drama, supplemented with affection. And if you're lucky, that affection won't run out as the years pass. I am completely free to work and play as I want in this creation they call earth."

The waitress came over with our waters and we asked for more time to select our food.

"What can you even get here veggie boy?" Ronnie said to me sarcastically.

Virgil jumped in. "You're a Vegetarian Mark?"

"Vegan actually. It's been about a year for me." I replied.

"Good for you." Virgil said as he smiled. "I've been Vegetarian since I was around your age and cut out the dairy about 10 years ago. I feel so much more alive, don't you?"

Ronnie burst into a big grin. "Well….I guess I'm the odd man out here. I'll just tuck my Vegan jokes in my back pocket." We all chuckled.

"I'll tell ya what though," I said, "I should call Mrs. Blank and let her know so she doesn't feed us all rabbit tomorrow."

Virgil had a look of shock. "What?"

"Yeah bro, this woman breeds, kills, and cooks rabbit in her backyard." Ronnie told Virgil, "It was actually good I must say...you guys are going to miss out!" He laughed.

Virgil had a look of disgust on his face.

"Actually..." I said. "Let me step outside and make that phone call now. If you remember Ronnie, she was upset that we didn't let her know I didn't eat meat. So I want to make sure she is aware ahead of time. If the waitress comes over, please order me a triple deck of pancakes with syrup, no butter."

Ronnie nodded...then grabbed my arm. "Hey man, make sure she still makes me some of that prime Bugs Bunny."

"That's so fucking wrong dude," I replied.

Mrs. Blank understood and informed me that she would make a meat-free stew for me and Virgil. I think she was just happy to be having company. As I hung up the phone, a car pulled up. It was Victoria! I noticed those beautiful eyes and hourglass-shaped figure from 50 feet away. I stayed outside awaiting her to get closer to me.

"Oh heeeey," She said in an awkward manner as she continued to walk closer.

"Hi Victoria. Do you remember me?"

She nodded her head, "Yes of course."

"Yeah, me and my film crew are here getting some grub." I replied, trying to make sure she knew I had a "crew."

She gave what seemed to be an uneasy smile and never really stopped to talk, just walked slowly. "Good. Listen, meet me in front of the bathrooms inside in about 3 minutes okay? I'm just going to drop my stuff off inside and I'll be there in a sec... oh...Please stay out here too for those 3 minutes if you wouldn't mind."

I agreed as she walked past me and entered through the door.

I stayed outside as she had requested. My mind wandered in different directions. Why would she want to talk to me there? Why wouldn't she just stop and talk to me here for a few minutes? Was she in a rush? Why the uneasy looking smile? Last time we met, she looked like she wanted to cuddle with me and have my babies. Maybe my ego was just messing with me. I felt really anxious to find out.

About 3 minutes passed, so I entered the door and went towards the bathrooms. There she was with a look of nervousness. She spoke softly.

"I'm sorry I couldn't stop and talk outside," she said with a concerned look, "To make a long story short, your project is causing much attention with the FBI or something. A man came to see me, and asked questions about what I told you guys about with Mrs. Blank. He said that it was important to his investigation. Apparently, he's working a long standing case on Mrs. Blank's husband."

My heart started racing as I was digesting her words. She looked so scared and concerned.

"He told me that you and your friend were trouble and were getting in his way. He said that I could be arrested if I associate myself with you guys. So, that's why I walked past you in a hurry. I don't know if I'm being watched. I'm scared. "

I looked down at the floor and shook my head slowly. "Wow, this is a lot. My partner said some man visited him too. I wonder if it's connected."

"I'm sorry Mark," she said, "I don't know what you got yourself into, but I can't be a part of it. Would you mind please leaving the diner with your crew... for me?"

"Yes of course." I said. I felt disappointed and scared. Disappointed that my chances with her were shot and then worried about this FBI agent guy.

"Thank you," she said, "And...I'm sorry. I would have liked to get to know you better." She touched my face, and walked away.

I got back to the booth and luckily the food had not come yet.

"Listen guys, we have to leave right now," I said, concerned.

Ronnie looked shocked, "Bro, what are you talking about?"

Unlike Ronnie, Virgil did not hesitate. He immediately got up and started making his way to the door.

"I'll explain in the car," I told Ronnie.

"Bro...What the fuck!?" Ronnie yelled after I filled them in. "I wonder if it was the same guy that visited me at the school!?"

"I noticed that you didn't even flinch, Virgil. You instantly got up and got to the car," I said.

"Yeah. I've been around long enough to know an urgent situation," Virgil continued, "I didn't need to know the reason. And Ronnie, next time something like this happens, ask questions later. It's important that you move fast in an urgent situation."

"Wait," Ronnie looked concerned, "So you're implying that there will be another urgent situation where we have to move fast bro?"

Virgil smirked, "Probably."

Ronnie's voice was turned up as he looked in the rear view mirror at Virgil. He spoke with emotion. "Okay...Fuck this. I want to know everything that's going on in your head! Why are you here? What do you think of this story we are putting on film? Are we in fucking danger?"

Virgil replied firmly, "Okay, well, I think you guys stumbled on an amazing discovery. I'm here to guide you to unearthing the mystery. Tomorrow we will finish it. However, I think it's important..." Virgil paused. Ronnie and I both anticipated his next words and explanation. He continued...

"That we stop and get something to eat. Are ya'll still hungry?"

Ronnie looked as though he wanted to punch Virgil in the face.

CHAPTER 14

The Monument

None of us said much at lunch. Ronnie did ask Virgil about the Guidestones once, but he said we would learn everything we needed to when we got there. He wasn't lying.

On the way to the hilltop that had the stones, I glanced over as we drove on the Hartwell Highway and saw them with my own eyes. What an amazing sight.

"There they are," Virgil said excitingly.

We got off on Guidestones Road, parked, got our equipment out, and walked to the site.

Incredible is an overused word. But that best describes what my eyes saw that day. This monument was the strangest and most amazing thing I had ever seen. Virgil couldn't stop grinning. He had a look as if he just got home after a long day's work. He was thrilled to be there and took in the moment.

"Okay. Let's set up a quality shot, so we can interview Virgil in front of the monument." I said.

I sound checked him, and Ronnie hit record…

ME: Please tell us who you are and your expertise to this project.

VIRGIL: My name is Virgil Riley, a truth-seeking journalist, and I've been studying the Georgia Guidestones for a little over a decade.

ME: Can you give the viewer a brief history of the Guidestones and what they are?

VIRGIL: The Guidestones were commissioned in 1979 by R. C. Christian. He hired the Elberton Granite Finishing Company to build the structure, here at the highest point in Elbert County. But as you can see, this is no average structure. At nearly 19 feet and 3 inches high, there is one slab in the center, with four arranged around it. They are astronomically aligned with the stars and each tablet has 10 guidelines inscribed. They are written in 12 different languages, four of which are ancient."

ME: Who is R.C. Christian?

VIRGIL: Nobody really knows who he is. There's no record of him. Some people believe he is part of a Luciferian religion and these monuments are for worship. Others believe that R.C. is part of the N.W.O. and these Guidelines are our new 10 Commandments after the apocalypse. And it's also been said that R.C. is of the Rosicrucian Order. But realistically, no one knows who R.C. Christian is. Not even the company that was hired to build it. They were basically paid specifically to not ask any questions. They have record of building it. In fact they have a smaller version at the Elberton Museum. However...If you go ask questions, they know nothing.

ME: I didn't know about the Guidestones. No one that I know of has heard about them. Why are they not talked about? This should be news...no?

VIRGIL: Well, I think maybe they are too new. We've heard about Stonehenge or the Lighthouse of Alexandria before, because those mysteries have been around a long time. These Guidestones were unveiled to the public in 1980. Supposedly, 100 people showed up to the unveiling. Of course, we have to wonder who those 100 people were. I think that adds to the mystery and adds to the conspiracy of R.C. Christian being a part of some sort of cult. But I think as people wake up and technology moves forward with social media and such, there will be no more hiding this monument. I heard that the radical radio host and filmmaker, Alex Jones was here shooting recently, so maybe he will have the Guidestones in one of his new documentaries. But I'm surprised the History Channel hasn't done a piece on it yet. I'm sure they will as we get closer to 2012 and that whole 'end of the world' hype starts getting heavier.

ME: Let's talk about the 10 guidelines. Do you think they are bad or good for society?"

VIRGIL: I think they're great for society. They make perfect sense and are reasonable. The human race has become out of control with reproduction and unnatural living. We've screwed up the food, the air, the water and the list goes on. The thing that strikes me as fascinating though, is that we really got bad in the 80's. You see, that's when cable TV, the microwave and the VCR took off. These inventions really brought us no good. We're now brainwashed by TV programming and TV commercials. Everyone is in a rush with microwave dinners and the tapings of their favorite shows. Chronic Illness has gone up. Cancer has gone up. And the population has gone up. The 80's is when all this was birthed, so it's ironic that these Guidestones were introduced in 1980. Or maybe it isn't irony.

ME: Why are the guidelines written in different languages?

VIRGIL: So everyone can read them. The creator clearly believes that everyone needs to read them. They're an important work.

ME: Who is the creator?

VIRGIL: I don't know for sure, but whoever it is has the right idea.

ME: So you don't think the creator is R.C. Christian?

VIRGIL: No, I'm sure he was just the person that carried out the order. And I'm sure it was under a fake identity.

ME: Why would they be lined up with the stars?

VIRGIL: The 4 outer stones are oriented to mark the limits of the 18.6 year lunar declination cycle. The center column features a hole through which the North Star can be seen regardless of time, as well as a slot that is aligned with the sun's solstices and equinoxes. A 7/8" aperture in the capstone allows a ray of sun to pass through at noon each day, shining a beam on the center stone indicating the day of the year. There are 3 alignments. One indicates the celestial pole. Another indicates annual travel of sun. And the third marks noontime throughout. It seems as though the purpose is to know time.

ME: Why would someone need to know time? Why can't we look at our watches or phones?

VIRGIL: But what happens when your watches and phones don't exist anymore? This astrologic monument will help humans without technology.

ME: Virgil, in your opinion, what is the point of this monument?

VIRGIL: Well, there is a time capsule buried 6 feet below on the left side of the tablet. It's clear to me, that between the astrological part, guideline part, languages part, and time capsule part... the Georgia Guidestones are meant to help man start over one day."

ME: You mentioned 2012 earlier. Do you think the apocalypse will happen then?

VIRGIL: No. I believe it to be more of a spiritual awakening for people. A mental shift. I think 2012 will cause a panic and make some good television. But make no mistake about it, it will be a great test for the elite to see how people react to some end of the world scenarios. Beta testing.

ME: Do you think that everything that's happened to Mrs. Blank is related to the Guidestones?

VIRGIL: I think that it's not a coincidence that Mrs. Blank lives in the same town as the Guidestones. I do think they are connected in some way, yes.

ME: How? What is the connection?

VIRGIL: Well, I don't want to say just yet. I need to get in the tunnel by the stream to see if I am correct.

ME: Is there anything else you want to add to this interview?

VIRGIL: No. I think we're good. Interview me again after I investigate the tunnel.

I signaled to Ronnie to turn the camera off.

"Bro, that was trippy man," Ronnie said to Virgil, "Dude, why would we have to start over? You think the Bible is correct?"

Virgil smiled. "I thought the interview was over?"

Ronnie looked like he wanted to punch him again.

"I'll tell you what though..." Virgil paused, as Ronnie and I anticipated something powerful to come out of Virgil's mouth.

"We need to make sure we bring a change of clothes for when we go into the stream and tunnel."

Ronnie had that look again.

I took the camera from Ronnie and started to capture B-roll of the Guidestones. As I slowly scanned the monument with the camera, I imagined Virgil's sound bites underneath my shots. It was great footage. Here I was, standing next to this amazing and mysterious monument getting quality shots. I glanced over at Ronnie and Virgil. They both touched and gazed at the Guidestones as if they were the most beautiful thing they had ever seen. I knew right then and there that I was making history.

THE GEORGIA GUIDESTONES
CENTER CLUSTER ERECTED MARCH 22 1980

BABYLONIAN CUNEIFORM

EGYPTIAN HIEROGLYPHIC

ASTRAL GREEK

LET THESE BE
GUIDESTONES
TO AN AGE
OF REASON

SANSKRIT

ASTRONOMIC FEATURES
1. GNOMEN STONE
2. CELESTIAL ALLEY
3. INDICATES

PHYSICAL
1. OVERALL HEIGHT
2. TOTAL WEIGHT
3. FOUR MAJOR

CHAPTER 15

The Plan

After breakfast, we loaded up the car with the equipment and made our way over to Mrs. Blank's farm. Virgil's idea was to go early and check out the stream and tunnel before lunch. He felt as though it would be beneficial to the project so he could ask Mrs. Blank's questions based on his findings.

"Okay guys, so here's the plan," Virgil's raspy voice rang out in the car.

"Only two of us should go into the tunnel. I'd like for one of you to stay up top and keep a look out."

"A look out?" Ronnie sounded off. "Bro, a look out for what? The owl? The police? What, are we stealing something!? Is this a fucking robbery!? Come on...a look out for what?"

I jumped in, "Calm down man, relax. Virgil has the experience and we're going to follow his lead. I will come down with you Virgil, and I'll get the footage needed. Ronnie you stay up top."

"Okay, so again...What am I looking out for?" Ronnie continued still letting the fear steer his emotions.

"Anything Ronnie." Virgil said, "Do you recall a man coming to visit you at your school?"

Virgil paused as Ronnie looked at him through the rearview mirror.

"And I know we remember Victoria's story of the so-called FBI agent coming to visit her. How about the officer that got fired for snooping at Mrs. Blank's? This is serious business boys. There are people out there that do NOT want you to discover something. I want you to wrap your heads around this concept. Accept it. Acceptance is powerful."

There's the acceptance thing again. That's what Hickenbottom said. Nerves ran through my body as I looked over at Ronnie. He looked like he was going to puke.

Virgil continued. "It is important that you guys stay calm and listen to my instructions at all times. Now...Mark, while we are in the tunnel you keep that camera on at all times. Don't turn it off for nothing. Plus, I'm going to need the added light from the camera to see. I brought a flashlight just in case though. Get as much raw footage as you can. Mic me up before we go in and I will give sound bites as we proceed. Ronnie, you stay up top and let us know if anything or anyone comes. But even more importantly, we may have to yell for you. There will be 3 code phrases, okay? The first one is 'Call the dry cleaners', that's going to mean call the police. The second is 'Pick up the groceries', that's going to mean come down and help us. And the last code is going to be 'Close up the store', and that is going to mean...Run. We will try our best to pop the tape out of the camera and throw it up to you if possible. When you get the tape, you take off. Do you understand?

Ronnie looked pale as a ghost as he just shook his head yes.

I was curious, "May I ask why the codes?"

"Same reason why they use codes on a football field. To disguise the play. If we're in one of the 3 situations, then we more than likely have an opponent, right? Well, these codes will at least throw them off and create more time, even if it's just 20 Seconds. It can help."

"I have one question,." Ronnie's voice trembled, "If we have to 'close up the store', what is my protocol? Run where?"

"I was getting to that. Hopefully we can throw the tape to you before you take off, but whatever you do, don't try and help us, just run as fast as you can. Now this goes for anyone that makes a break for it...Listen close. Don't even bother with the car. You're always more elusive on foot. You can troop it through people's backyards and such. Get back to the Days Inn where we are staying. Out back behind the building, there is a bush. I marked it with a small purple ribbon. It may take a few minutes to find it, but it's there. To the left of that bush I buried 3 copies of the Elberton Enigma DVD. It's only about 6 inches deep and it's soft dirt. You can dig it up with your hands if you need to."

"Wow you made copies huh?" I said.

"Yes," Virgil replied "I want you to understand. The DVDs combined with this new footage is priority. Make sure that what we shoot today is on the same tape as yesterday with the Guidestones. That footage needs to come out of this at all costs, and it needs to been seen by as many people as possible. So Ronnie.... and or Mark, if you have to escape....go get the DVD copies, make your way to a train or bus station and leave town for at least a month."

Ronnie let out a roar. "A month!?"

"Yes," Virgil continued, "A month at least, to figure out your situation. After 30 days, you'll have to make a decision on whether to come back to your life or stay on the run. You get yourself to a hotel or motel outside of Georgia if you can. Use cash always. Never credit, debit or check. If you go past the month, then try and find something more secretive on Craigslist. Maybe a room for rent or even a hostel. Keep moving. Few months here, few months there. Don't contact your family. But if you feel you really need to, you can write a letter by good ol' fashioned snail mail. Do not send directly to your parents though, you send it to a friend first. Not a best friend, but a friend you trust, one that you don't get to see too often. You know, someone that would be inconspicuous by the authorities. In the letter, you tell the friend to hand-deliver it to your family at a restaurant or public place of your choice. I only suggest doing this once if you feel you need to. Never more than once. It's just enough to let them know that you are okay. Never give your location under any circumstance. Always keep your finger on the pulse of the news, specifically in Georgia and of course the alternative topic websites. You need to always be up on your intel. Knowing may keep you alive. Again, after your first month, you have to make a judgement call."

Ronnie glanced over at me.

"Okay...I guess this is the big time Mark! Netflix here we come," he spoke loud and sarcastically.

I gave a nervous chuckle.

Virgil wasn't done.

"And FYI. These codes go for anytime. Not just with the tunnel. I want us to be prepared for all that happens. Remember, the most important factor in all of this, is the footage. The footage must survive at all costs. The truth must be exposed to as many people as possible. You didn't come all this way for nothing boys."

My head felt like it was spinning. This was a lot of information and speculation all in one breath. "My plan was to edit all this new footage into the original documentary." I said.

"I'm aware of that Mark, but it just may not be a reality. But it's important that the DVD and the new footage gets out to the public. Even if separately. But boys, understand that these are just precautions. Plan B if you will. Plan A is walking out of Mrs. Blank's today with great footage. And Mark putting together a great film to sell. Right?"

For the remainder of the ride to Mrs. Blanks, I couldn't help but overthink everything Virgil instructed us to do. What did he know that we didn't? What did he expect to happen? Was my life about to change? Or is Virgil just a conspiracy theorist who has done a little too much research? I mean, he took it as far as to bury copies of the DVD and created code phrases for us. This guy went all out for his 'Plan B'.

Regardless if Virgil was a nut job or not, we were going in that tunnel shortly. That was reality. My palms were clammy. I rubbed them on my jeans as the anticipation and anxiety roared. I knew I needed to relax so I could focus on the job at hand. If I want to be a great documentary filmmaker, facing fears will be part of the job. 'Plan A' was in full effect. I blocked 'Plan B' out of my head and glanced over at Ronnie as he drove the car. He still looked like he wanted to Puke. I glanced back to Virgil, his eyes were closed and looked to be meditating or something. I followed suit and closed my eyes as I focused on my breaths. We would be pulling up to

Mrs. Blank's shortly. I wondered what Dr. Hickenbottom would say right now.

CHAPTER 16

The Stream

"It's a pleasure to meet you Virgil," Mrs. Blank said as she shook his hand, "I'm really hoping to get some answers today."

"Well, I hope I can provide those for you Mrs. Blank. The food smells great," Virgil replied.

"Yes. Yes. I made potato and carrot stew for you and Mark. I think you will enjoy it. And of course...Ronnie and I will indulge in some rabbit deluxe."

"I can't wait!" Ronnie said excitingly, I could tell he was acting because he was so nervous.

"So, the food won't be ready for another 30 Minutes or so. Would you all like to have a seat and I can serve you biscuits?"

"Mrs. Blank," I put my hand on her shoulder, "If it's okay with you, I'm going to take this time to set up the camera, tripod, and lights at the dinner table. We're going to go to the tunnel first, but when we come back and sit down to eat, I want to be ready to capture Virgil giving you your answers. I want to shoot it all as real as possible. So it's important that everything is set up beforehand."

She nodded in agreement. "Wow, I can't believe you are really going in that tunnel. I'm so anxious!" She looked at Virgil with a sad face. "Mr. Riley, I just want to know why my husband and son were taken from me. You understand that right?"

He had a look of compassion. "I'm going to do my best Mrs. Blank."

About 10 minutes had passed and the lighting and tripod was all set to go at the dinner table. I mic'd up Virgil with a lavaliere and as I did we caught eye contact. Compassion dripped from his eye sockets. He put his hand on my shoulder.

"Are you ready Mark?" He asked sternly.

I nodded my head yes. We informed Mrs. Blank we would be back anywhere between 20 and 45 minutes. We grabbed Ronnie's backpack which had our second pair of pants and socks as we made our way out the back door.

The walk to the back was the most anxiety-driven 2 or 3 minutes of my life. None of us spoke. What else was there to say? Virgil said everything he needed to back in the dark ride over.

We made our way through the brush as we heard the stream getting louder and louder with every step we took.

No matter how freaked out one could be, seeing the beauty of the stream relaxed me. The sound, the view, the feeling. It was as though positive energy flowed from it.

"Alright boys, let's change into our tunnel clothes." Virgil said.

After getting a new pair of jeans and socks on, we all put on our boots. Of course Ronnie did the same under the assumption that he might have to come help us.

"Alright, let's do this." I said. "I'm turning the camera on now."

Virgil led the way by placing his right foot into the clear flowing stream. The water seemed to be a tad over a foot deep and went up almost to Virgil's knee. With one foot in, he turned around to me with a serious face.

"Remember, don't turn that record button off until we're back. And boys...The footage is priority."

We both nodded. Ronnie and I made eye contact as I was about to put my first leg in the stream. He gave me a salute sign as if to wish me luck.

The water was warm and actually felt relaxing. I went into filmmaker mode. I was all about 'Plan A' and getting the best footage I could. I got shots of the stream and made sure I was about 10 feet behind Virgil to capture his journey. This part of the film was all about Virgil going through this tunnel and reporting on what he finds. That was my focus.

As we approached the entrance of the tunnel, I turned on my camera light. This lit up the darkness ahead beautifully.

Virgil was now about 10 feet in the tunnel and I was just entering. He turned around to the camera.

"So here we are, just entering this mysterious tunnel. I'm expecting the unexpected for sure, but convinced that we will find an abundance of gold based on the fact that golden nuggets have been found on Mrs. Blank's property. You can also see the occasional golden nugget embedded in the stream floor."

Just at that moment, we heard hooting, like that of an owl. Virgil and I both turned around to look. My camera picked up Ronnie looking up at the top of the Bridge. Ronnie didn't say anything, but he pointed to where the owl was. I turned my camera back to Virgil.

"I was expecting the owl. It's only keeping guard. Let's keep moving." He then yelled over to Ronnie, "Don't worry about him, just don't stare at it!"

With every step we took in the stream we had to go slow, one foot in front of the other, catching our balance as the stream was clearly descending downhill.

Virgil turned his head back to the camera. "It's important that we do not fall down. We don't know how steep this stream goes and we certainly don't want to slide down on our backs."

About another 10 or 15 feet in, Virgil pointed to the left of us. I was amazed. There was hieroglyphs on the wall!

"I had a feeling these would be here. These are ancient drawings similar to what you would find in the Middle East. Ahh, look to your right. There's your owl."

Low and behold, on the right was a drawing of an owl on the wall.

"Owls are thought to be supreme surveillance creatures. They can fly high and low. Their vision and hearing is superb. They automatically see what they hear and hear what they see and can track the smallest of movements. Each with dead accurate, real time, distance, elevation and direction target parameters. The connection is clear. Whoever drew these picture on these walls, uses owls as surveillance systems."

I scanned the walls with my camera, picking up this incredible footage. Up ahead on the left was another interesting image. Virgil excitedly started describing it.

"This one is familiar. You see you have 3 small people standing in front of a bigger man sitting on a throne. This man is much bigger because if he stood up off his chair he would be gigantic compared to the other 3. Then, in between them is some sort of 'wheel device' on a table and in the 'wheel device' there is an image of the Sun. This picture was originally found in Iran which is believed to be ancient Sumeria. Whoever put these drawings here were either good copycat artists or were on the same page with the original artists."

We continued down the stream carefully as I got the shots of the drawings on the walls.

"Ahh, look down!" Virgil yelled out as his voice echoed down the tunnel.

I pointed the camera down and low and behold, there were a bunch of small golden nuggets at the bottom of the stream. They looked to be lodged into the ground and clumped together.

Virgil looked at the camera and smiled, "We're getting closer."

As we went down further, I shot more of the drawings on the wall. There were bird people, horse people, monkey people and lots of what could be described as spaceships. There were drawings of large people next to small people. Lots of cone and pyramid shapes throughout. Virgil looked like a kid in the candy store. He beamed with excitement.

As I was getting these shots, I heard the sounds of massive amounts of water flowing together. Just ahead we stumbled upon something that I have never seen before. Virgil went back into narrator mode.

"Okay, now this is fascinating...as you can clearly see, this is where the stream stops! But there is a very precisely built hole in the floor which is acting as a drain. This drain looks to be about a foot or so in diameter. Hey! And there goes another one, about 15 feet ahead....and there is another one too! The other ones are probably to help get the water that the first one missed. You can clearly hear the water slapping through the drain and splashing below. My guess is this dumps into a larger pool of water. So essentially we are standing on top of an engineered, man-made waterfall."

I got great shots of these 3 drains. As I scanned ahead, I noticed that the stream was now gone and the floor flowed with...gold! It was a golden floor!

"Well will you look at that," Virgil said enthusiastically, "The floor is made up of lots of gold. Now normally in a gold mine, you have to do tons of digging and scraping just to get a little nugget of gold. But clearly not here! There is a massive amounts of gold...enough to see the color of it glow. My guess is that this is monoatomic gold. Powerful stuff."

Virgil picked up a golden nugget and turned around to the camera to speak to the audience.

"I'm going to take a wild stab and say that someone with great technology stopped this stream from flowing further by creating a draining system. This of course exposes the gold nuggets in the floor and makes them easy to locate. And look ahead. It's like the yellow brick road. This is amazing! You have to wonder how far this tunnel goes."

My intuition was kicking in that we should go back.

"Hey man, maybe we should go back. I mean, Ronnie is waiting and probably worried. We found what we were looking for. And there is no way we could throw this tape to Ronnie if we had to right?"

I could tell Virgil wanted to keep going. "Yeah. You're right. Who knows how far this tunnel goes anyway. This thing may go all the way to Florida for all we know. I'll have to come back another day to go further. Let's head back."

I reached down to put some gold in my pockets.

"No! No!" Virgil yelled out, "Don't do that, that's stealing."

I squinted my face.

"It doesn't belong to you Mark. Let's go."

I couldn't help but wonder who it belonged to.

Going back upstream was not easy, especially with a heavy camera! Virgil advised me to put the mini DV tape in my pocket in case I dropped the camera. So much for pause-free recording…

We were both exhausted when we got back up to the top of the Tunnel. As we went from the darkness to the natural sunlight I immediately noticed Ronnie was not there.

"Ronnie!" I yelled out.

"Sssshhhhh!" Virgil put his finger over his mouth to shush me. "Either he's back in the house with Mrs. Blank, or he decided we were down there too long and went to 'close the store'. Let's change our clothes back and continue with 'Plan A'. The footage is priority. Let's go give Mrs. Blank her answers."

Now I wanted to punch him in the face. "What answers? We didn't find any answers."

"Sure we did," Virgil replied.

I felt my stomach drop at the thought of Ronnie running off. I scanned the area looking for that creepy fucking owl.

CHAPTER 17

The Explanation

"I hope you boys are hungry!" Mrs. Blank yelled to us as we got closer to the back porch.

There was an image behind her, and it became clear that it was Ronnie! I was thrilled to see him! He came running over to us.

"Bro, thank goodness you guys made it! You wouldn't believe what happened to me. What did you guys find?" He was all hyped up and excited.

"Hand us our bags please?" Virgil asked. "Let's get changed while we swap stories real quick."

"Our findings are pretty simple. There were ancient drawings on the walls of the tunnel, and eventually the stream stopped and went down a man-made drain. Almost the whole floor was made of gold! What happened to you man?"

"Gold!? Lots of it!?" Ronnie loudly asked.

"Billions of dollars easy, assuming the tunnel kept going," Virgil said.

"My story isn't so simple I suppose." Ronnie was revved up like he drank 10 energy drinks. "That damn owl didn't budge...."

"Wait!" Virgil said, "Mark you should record this."

"Good Idea," I said. I took the tape out from my pocket and placed back in the camera. "Start from the top Ronnie and be as descriptive as you can."

I didn't even bother to mic him up, I just pointed the camera at him and he continued.

"While I was waiting for you guys in the tunnel, the owl showed up. It just sat there and stared at me. I tried not to make eye contact. Then, maybe 3 to 5 minutes after you guys went in the tunnel, the owl flew over to me and landed a few feet in front of me." Ronnie paused. "I know this sounds nuts....but...Then it spoke to me."

"Really? What did it say?" Virgil asked.

Ronnie looked pale. "It doesn't have to be this way," He paused again, "That's what it said...It doesn't have to be this way."

"Be what way?!" I yelled.

Ronnie looked puzzled. "Bro, I don't know. All I know is that I was spooked out pretty bad. The owl flew off, and I ran back to the house. I'm so sorry guys. I abandoned you when you needed me. I was just really scared at that moment. I ran through the brush at full speed. Look at my arms, they're cut up a little from the prickers."

"Don't worry about it," Virgil said, "Everything is good now, and that's all that matters."

Ronnie nodded.

"I just have one question. What did the owl sound like?"

"Bro, I don't really know how to describe it. Kind of like a muffled robot or something."

"Did you tell Mrs. Blank?" Virgil asked.

"No. I didn't want to spook her. We actually started to eat a little while ago. She's been telling me stories about her son. I was just hoping that you guys would come back. Thank God you did!"

Ronnie gave me and Virgil a hug. The look in his eye was that of someone who almost got into a major car accident. I've seen people like that before and that's the only thing I can compare this to. He was shook up, but seemed very grateful to be alive and well. Virgil and I put on our dry jeans, socks, and shoes and entered the house with Ronnie. I guess it's time to capture the last part of this documentary.

Mrs. Blank served us all our plates of stew. I placed the camera on the tripod and plugged it into the wall to charge it up.

"Okay guys, here is how this part is going to go. Ronnie you're on camera. We're basically going to have a three-way conversion at the dinner table while we're eating. Virgil will lead the way as he is the one with the information and opinions. Mrs. Blank, I'm sure you will have plenty of questions to ask him. I will be in it too so I can ask questions as well.

Everyone nodded their heads. I began to mic the three of us up and perform a sound check with Ronnie. It was time to finish this thing. Finally. The camera was on…

ME: Okay. Virgil why don't you let Mrs. Blank know what we found in the tunnel and what your thoughts are...

VIRGIL: Mrs. Blank, that is…. a very special tunnel. The first thing to note is that we noticed gold nuggets embedded in the floor of the stream. As we got deeper, there were ancient drawings on the walls of the tunnel. From my experience, most of them were from Sumerian times from the Mesopotamian area, which is in the Middle-East. The Sumerians were supposedly the first organized human civilization on earth. The Sumerians actually had an organized society. They had schools, calendars, politicians, farms, tools, jobs you name it. The big mystery is how they came about. It's called the 'missing link'. In other words, how did we go from a prehistoric cave man to a well-oiled machine of a society? And go back further than that, how did we go from primate to caveman? Regardless of what anyone believes or speculates...The important question is, how the heck did these ancient drawings end up in a small tunnel in Elberton, Georgia?

MRS. BLANK: Okay...

VIRGIL: Well, I think I know. As we continued through the downhill tunnel we got to a point where the water went down a drain.

MRS. BLANK: A drain? Like in a bathtub?

VIRGIL: Yes. A bigger version. It was built and built well. There were 3 drains actually. We could not see much below, but we could hear the water. Clearly it's another stream or body of water of some sort. Either way, the water was redirected for a purpose. And that purpose was to have access to the gold. The further down the tunnel, the more gold was in the floor. I mean, it was shining and glowing, that's how much gold is there. Without the water flowing over the floor, it makes it easier to dig out the nuggets of gold. We're talking trillions of dollars here! We don't know how far the tunnel goes because we turned around. I've never seen so much natural gold in my life.

MRS. BLANK: Well...That would explain my son then. He never

talked about the tunnel much, but I always wondered how he bought all his drugs. Not to mention he bought a car when he turned 19! He told me he worked a job in Florida, but didn't give much information about it. I was suspicious. I figured maybe he was a drug dealer, but he never was in trouble to my knowledge. Maybe he took gold and sold it?"

VIRGIL: That is very possible Mrs. Blank, yes.

ME: So, who put the drawings on the walls of the tunnel? Who made the drains? And how are the Guidestones connected to all of this Virgil?

MRS. BLANK: Yes, these Guidestones that you told me about on the phone...I had no idea they were even in this town.

VIRGIL: It is in my opinion, that R.C. Christian was a cover up identity and was instructed by the Anunnaki to have the Georgia Guidestones constructed.

ME: What is Anunnaki?

VIRGIL: The Anunnaki are a highly intelligent race of extraterrestrials supposedly from the planet Nibiru. They look similar to us, except they are more reptilian skinned, much taller, and the back of their skulls are longer. I believe that they came to Earth 450,000 years ago in search of gold. You see, gold is not worth money to them like it is to us. Monatomic gold is a high form of energy to them. They break it down and use it. Kind of like how we use gasoline. It's said that they got fed up with putting in so much work digging up gold, so they decided to work smarter not harder. They needed workers. One of these scientists started playing around with DNA experiments. He spliced Anunnaki DNAs with different animals. One animal that was of interest to them was the primates because of the similarities. It took a long time to get it right. This may be the reason why there are so many hybrid creatures in ancient drawings. The man-horse, the bird-man and such. In fact, these experiments may have been the birth of Bigfoot. It's arguable.

ME: Wow, but that kind of makes sense. How else would there be so many large, hairy, human-like, monkey men spotted across the world? And if they are of this Alien race you're talking about, that would be why they're very smart. I mean, these creatures are elusive and hard to catch right?

VIRGIL: Indeed. Some say their experiments with primates may have led to early cavemen. The overly hairy human with no speaking language. Some even say that the caveman was already here and the Anunnaki did experiments on them to create us. Either way, they are responsible for speeding up our evolution and it didn't happen overnight. There were many errors. But finally, they got it right and created man...what we are today. This process is similar to what we did with dogs. We genetically created them from wolves. Then we domesticated them. Also look at how many breeds of dogs there are. That explains why humans can be white, black, Asian, etc. You can cross-breed.

MRS. BLANK: Aliens? Really? Mr Riley...Come on! This sounds like a bad movie. Why would these creatures care so much to have the Guidestones created to help us start over? It doesn't make sense.

VIRGIL: As the story goes, there were two brothers. Enki and Enlil. They were both sons of the leader and God Anu who ruled from the planet Nibiru. Enki and Enlil were sent to earth to lead these missions. One of them became very attached to the humans and looked at us as his sons and his creations. And the other brother was colder and looked at us as slaves to get the job done. This started a conflict. It's your classic good versus evil story. Some could even argue the analogy of God versus the devil.

MRS. BLANK: Okay, so you're saying that God and the devil could have come from these two...brothers from another planet who rivaled each other? So that would explain the Garden of Eden? The talking snake that tricked Eve? A snake is a reptilian, right?

VIRGIL: That's correct. Just speculation of course though.

MRS. BLANK: No offense, but this sounds crazy. Like a fairy tale!

VIRGIL: I understand your doubt Mrs. Blank. But allow me to continue with the fairy tale. When the Anunnaki got their gold and left, some stayed to help build human society. In text they were called 'The Watchers'. They were considered 'Gods' amongst men. They were bigger, stronger, and smarter. The good ones taught humans how to farm, make tools, and create civilization. Most of them viewed us as their creations. Again, back to the dog example. We love dogs, right? But there are some humans that do not like dogs. They take up dog fighting or they torture dogs and what not. Well, the Anunnaki are no different. There were some who didn't treat us well. Many of them would mate with human women, this created what we call 'Demi Gods'. And these children were more advanced than regular humans. You can see a lot of examples of all this in Greek mythology, Hercules being the most famous one.

ME: Hey what about vampires?

VIRGIL: Great question. I think it's extremely possible that Vampires did and or do exist and were another experiment gone bad. They're similar to cold-blooded reptilians. Some have called vampires the 'Fallen Ones' and some have called them the

'Shining Ones'. The Annunaki were also described in similar terms in many texts. The biggest and maybe most important text being the 'Book of Enoch' which was removed from the Bible. In this book, Anunnaki were referred to as 'The Fallen'. In one part of the book it says, "When they turned themselves against men, in order to devour them" and also, "…and began to injure birds, beasts, reptiles, and fishes, to eat their flesh one after another, and to drink their blood." The Book of Enoch reveals that vampires could have originated from the offspring of the union between 'The Watchers' and the human women. When the children of the watchers had consumed all of the food available, they turned to mankind and began to eat their flesh and drink their blood. There really isn't many recorded eras that don't have myths or legends about nocturnal humans with fangs that suck blood. These stories were around centuries before Bram Stoker ever wrote the Dracula story.

ME: So where does the Illuminati or elite fit into all this? That's what I'd like to know.

VIRGIL: The Anunnaki eventually had to leave earth, so they placed "watchers" in the shadows to guide us. The problem is, because they were split up in their views, two organizations eventually formed. Ones who wanted humans to be controlled, and others who wanted humans to thrive. These two organizations have

the bloodline, and the enlightenment. But when you are

enlightened and awake, you have powers, and these powers can be used for good...or bad. The best example I can give is the 'Star Wars' movies. There were the Jedis and the Siths. They both had the power of the force, but they used it differently. Believe me, George Lucas was informing us right in front of our own eyes. One of those groups is what got those Guidestones built and placed the message for us to read. They are giving us the knowledge to start over and do it right. By doing this, they are also insinuating that something will happen to end most of our civilization. And the other side, well not only are they manipulating humans down the wrong path, but they may be the ones protecting that tunnel of gold out back.

ME: Interesting. So if there was an end...When would it happen? And how?

VIRGIL: I don't know when. But as far as how...I would guess a massive natural disaster such as a super volcano or a solar flare. Such a cataclysmic event would cause our technology to be swept away and humans would become like wild animals. In survival mode, we would become vicious toward each other. Many would rape, steal and kill while others would die from famine and disease. Bottom line, the population would decrease.

ME: Yeah but, if the other side wanted us gone, or downsized, why wouldn't they do it themselves? Why would they need Mother

Nature to contribute?

VIRGIL: They already did do it. They did their jobs, Mark. We're reliant on technology, we are overpopulated, and we are in poor health. If they have the advanced knowledge of something coming, such as a storm, then all they had to do was their job before the so-called deadline. Knowing is power, right? That's why the Government has the CIA. That's why Fortune 500 companies do their due diligence before buying another company. Intel is king. Let me ask you this...How many people will be at a disadvantage without the luxuries of technology? People don't even know how to read maps anymore because of GPS. How would they communicate with their aunt that's across the country? What would people do without TV? Cars? Shoot...Electricity as a whole? Let's dig further. How many obese people will survive in a new world where you have to climb, run, and jump? How many people with illnesses would survive when their meds run out?

ME: Holy shit…You're right.

VIRGIL: The folks that have prepared themselves spiritually, physically and mentally will have the best chance at survival. And of course their families, assuming they prepared for them.

ME: But how would the 'powers that be' even know when Mother Nature was gonna hit?

VIRGIL: A few ways. For one, if they are led by the other side's direction, then their Annunaki watchers can predict it. They have more advanced technology than us. Forget all this Doppler system stuff you see on the five o'clock news, they can predict earthquakes, never mind hurricanes. And secondly, there is HAARP.

ME: HAARP? Dare I ask?

VIRGIL: It stands for High-Frequency Active Auroral Research Program. Its purpose is to analyze the ionosphere and investigate the potential for developing ionospheric enhancement technology for radio communications and surveillance. The HAARP program operates in a major sub-arctic facility, named the HAARP Research Station, on an air force–owned site in Alaska. Many believe they can use this technology to create weather. Hurricanes, volcanoes, earthquakes and rain, all of which can be used to control population.

Mrs. Blank: I don't know how much of this I can believe. What does rain have to do with anything?

Virgil: Rain is a big part. What they do is spray chemicals in the sky. We call them chemtrails. You can see lines of smoke sometimes in the sky. You can tell the difference because contrails which come from a plane, disappear and chemtrails stay for a while. Sometimes you can look up and see lines upon lines in the sky. They usually spray right before a rain storm. The rain brings the chemicals down upon us.

Me: I've heard about this! The chemicals can cause all sorts of harm on people. Like Alzheimer's right?

Virgil: Correct. Some say chronic illnesses and fatigue too. It's a very precise method in harming us, because they can pick a city and go to work. And the average person, doesn't really look up, so no one even notices.

Me: Is this HAARP machine alien technology?

Virgil: All our technology is alien because Annunaki were first. Something like the microwave is old to them. But yes, the other side's watchers passed the knowledge down to create HAARP. I believe they started in Norway. They created an ionospheric heater called EISCAT. There, scientists pioneered exploration of the ionosphere by perturbing it with radio waves in the 2–10 MHz range, and studying how the ionosphere reacts. HAARP in Alaska came about in 1993. It's funded by the U.S. Government and some big corporations. Of course you know who's pulling the strings.

ME: The other side, as you call them. Hmmm. So, you think that it's no accident that the Guidestones were built in the same town as this tunnel filled with massive amounts of gold....which also have ancient Anunnaki drawings on the wall.

VIRGIL: Exactly. There's a lot of gold in there. And it's probably high powered monoatomic gold. The Anunnaki wanting the Guidestones to be in Elberton could very well mean that this area on earth is filled with gold! I would assume it's not just that one strip of tunnel. It can very well be the whole town. This whole town may have gold underneath it. We didn't continue through the tunnel so it's hard to say. But if we kept going we would have discovered a lot more answers. Maybe even a spaceship of some sort. Maybe even an ET or ET artifacts.

ME: So you think these extraterrestrials could be down there?

VIRGIL: Could be, but I doubt it. The ones that are here and leading the other side are probably hidden in a cave somewhere more isolated or deep down in the core of the earth. But maybe a spaceship was found by humans and it's kept down there? Who knows? This tunnel is exclusive. Scientists, archaeologists, scholars...they would have a field day if they found it! It would change the landscape of our economy. It would change everything. What would the government do with all that money? How would they explain the drains? The drawings? Could you imagine it on the five o'clock news?

ME: So this is why the footage we got is so important?

VIRGIL: Yes

MRS. BLANK: Virgil...I have to ask. In your opinion, how did my son and husband die?

VIRGIL: Well, I believe that they both got too close to the gold

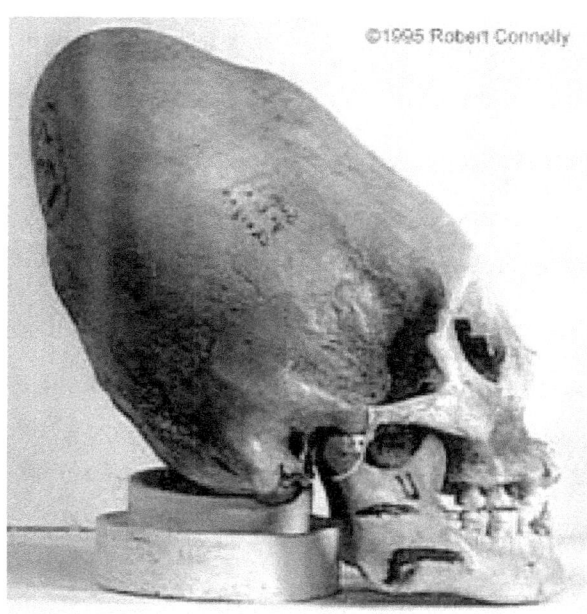

©1995 Robert Connolly

and needed to be terminated. Call it collateral damage.

MRS. BLANK: By this other side you speak of?

VIRGIL: Yes.

ME: Illuminati?

VIRGIL: That's a name for it. But the organization that knows about this discovery in Elberton probably has an exclusive secret agency working for them. We made light of this agency in the Will Smith movie 'Men In Black'. That's what Hollywood does...They take something serious and make it playful and silly. The public is conditioned to view it as Sci-Fi (science fiction).

ME: Are you saying that the guy who came to visit Ronnie and then Veronica was probably an MIB?

VIRGIL: Yes. There is probably a small group of them that are assigned to this property because that tunnel is an entrance to the gold and whatever else is down there. Their mission is to NOT let that gold be discovered at any cost. And on top of all that, maybe they are waiting for the Anunnaki to come back? Or maybe they are in cahoots with some of them? We won't ever know. Again, we turned around and didn't go deeper into that tunnel. But Mrs. Blank, your husband and son were probably murdered by the other side. You said your husband was going to be cutting down the brush with a chainsaw? Well, that may have forced them to take immediate action. And if your son went back there often without you knowing, they probably let him live because he became a drug addict. But as you told us, one day he got upset and went out there in a rage with a gun and never returned. They had to do what they had to do.

MRS. BLANK: This is a lot to grasp.

VIRGIL: I know...I'm sorry Mrs. Blank. But I also believe that they were responsible for the officer getting fired who wanted to investigate the gold. He was a potential problem, so they threatened the chief of police to pull the string.

MRS. BLANK: Okay, but what about my dog....?

VIRGIL: Yes, I believe they kidnapped your dog and used technology that we can't explain to mute him because his barking was causing too much attention. Maybe they have been doing more extensive work than usual out back? The barking would eventually blow their cover? Or it just annoyed them?

ME: What about her being a so-called witch?

VIRGIL: I believe they manipulated the town into believing that you were a witch. This image of you would help keep people away from your property. It also caused your son to not have friends to come over and play due to kids being investigative and curious. The other side was protecting the tunnel at the expense of you and your family.

MRS. BLANK: This is nuts.

ME: So they had to sacrifice this poor woman to follow through with the mission of protecting that tunnel.

VIRGIL: Correct.

ME: So the dog losing its voice box could have been to further Mrs. Blank being perceived a certain way?

VIRGIL: That's a solid assumption. Good call. It brought on the Inquirer national story. I'm assuming you can't move away very easy now can you? They need you to live here Mrs. Blank.

ME: What about the owl?

VIRGIL: The owl, like the dog's surgery is fancy technology at work. My guess is, that owl is a drone.

MRS. BLANK: A drone?

VIRGIL: Yes, a robot. Owls don't come out during the day time. I have a feeling that owl is the eyes and ears of the group of agents that watch over this property and town. It probably feeds back video and audio to them, wherever they are.

ME: So that's how the owl spoke to Ronnie?

MRS. BLANK: The owl spoke?

VIRGIL: Yeah...It said…

At that very moment…It looked as though some sort of lightbulb went off in Virgil's head. Like something just dawned on him. His face looked as though he was worried. He signaled to Mrs. Blank to get him a piece of paper and a pen. But why didn't he just ask out loud? Then he continued to speak...

VIRGIL: The owl said that...It didn't have to be this way….Which is why we...Ummm, yeah we should not put this documentary out. It's just too dangerous.

"What!?" Ronnie yelled from behind the camera.

I could tell something was wrong by the way Virgil was stalling to talk as he awaited the pen and paper from Mrs. Blank.

VIRGIL: Yes Ronnie, this agency is no one to play with. They will hurt you and destroy your life to protect this secret.

Mrs. Blank placed the pen and paper in front of him. Virgil give me a signal to talk as he wrote down something. I started to understand where he was going with this and realized what was happening. I signaled Ronnie to cut the tape off and pop it out. I put my finger over my mouth to signal to him to be quiet.

ME: "Aaaaah yeah, I think I agree. Too dangerous. In fact we should just ditch this tape all together."

Virgil held up the piece of paper for me to see. It read...

"They're listening to us. Give Ronnie and I a blank tape to put in our pockets. After that, it's time for you and Ronnie to close up the store. I'll stay behind with her. Move slow and quiet out of the house, but when you get outside, RUN!"

My heart started thumping. Ronnie couldn't see the paper from that distance, so I had to rely on him following my lead. Mrs. Blank didn't read it either. Virgil's intention was probably to keep her calm. I stood up, trying my best to not make any noise. I went to my bag and pulled out three blank Mini DV tapes. I begin to understand the point. If caught, there was a chance they would think that was the main tape from today. Knowing Virgil, it was his way of giving someone a few seconds to break free. I gave one to Virgil and Ronnie. Of course Ronnie was confused. I signaled for him to put it in his pocket.

"So, why don't you guys go get washed up for dinner." Virgil told us. "All this crazy talk and we haven't even eaten yet. So Mrs. Blank, tell me about your husband, when did you meet him?"

Mrs. Blank smiled and started to tell Virgil about him. I knew that was me and Ronnie's cue. I signaled for him to follow me, as I took the camera off the tripod. We slowly walked to the front door. I turned around to glance back at Virgil and Mrs. Blank, and Damien was barking. Virgil waved his hands to me as if to say...Hurry up!

We took a few steps off the front porch. I signaled to Ronnie to keep it down and I whispered to him. "We have to close the store," he handed me the main tape and I put in my left pocket. The blank tape was in the right.

"I guess that means we can't take my car," Ronnie whispered.

I shook my head no. I placed the camera in the front bush thinking I could always come back for it if there was chance. As I was placing it in the bush, we heard loud noises inside like people were stomping and moving around. I knew what the sounds meant. Ronnie and I took off running down the dirt road. We didn't get far before we heard a really loud and terrorizing scream. It was Virgil. At that moment, I knew that he just took one for the team. He had sacrificed himself to slow down the agency people so we could get away. I was terrified.

As we were running I heard sounds and energy flying by us. It was bullets being shot from a gun with a silencer. Just as Ronnie said "What's that?" It happened. A burst of blood spurted from his leg. He was hit! He screamed in pain as he fell to the ground.

"Leave me!" Tears flooded his eyes, but he spoke seriously. "Protect the footage. We didn't come all this way for nothing bro!"

Before I could make a decision a man in all black caught up to us. He looked to be wearing black cargo pants and a long black thermal shirt. He had a black ski mask on and had a walkie talkie hanging from his belt. He was gasping for air and stopped about 15 feet in front of us. We were at gunpoint.

"Mr. Calloway... Mr. Simmons... It didn't have to be this way. I just need the footage. Pass over the tape, and you can go home."

Ronnie was in agony, holding his leg as the blood gushed out profusely.

"What about his leg? If I give you the tape, what happens?" I asked

"You call an ambulance, say someone shot him and ran off. You didn't see who it was. You never show that documentary again, and no one ever sees the footage on that tape. No harm done."

"How can I trust you?" I asked still trying to catch my breath.

"You can't," The man said, "But the other option is I just shoot you both dead and take the tape."

I felt calm for some reason. I made eye contact with Ronnie. I reached into my right pocket and took out the tape. I threw it on the ground next to where Ronnie was lying.

"There are two tapes. The other one is in his pocket." I said.

The man walked over slow still holding the gun. He reached down and picked up the tape and put in his pocket. Then he frisked Ronnie looking for the other tape. He felt it in his pocket and out of nowhere Ronnie kicked him in the balls with his good leg! As soon as he did that I leapt forward and kicked him in the chest as hard as I could knocking him over as he clenched his gonads.

"Run!" Ronnie yelled. And I did. I ran as fast as I could. I knew it wouldn't be long before shots would be fired, so I quickly hooked a left into the woods. For a good 10 or 15 minutes I just ran as hard as I could, letting adrenaline guide me.

Finally, I stopped and dropped to my knees. I did my best to think clearly. I have never worked my body that hard in my life. My heart felt like it was going to come out of my chest. My ears kept popping, almost as if I just got out of a pool. Sweat dribbled down my forehead. I was a terrified mess.

As tears flooded my eyes, I came to the conclusion that if I was going to make it out of here, I would have to think carefully...strategically. Adrenaline would not be enough. I pushed my fear to the side. I pushed my sorrow for Virgil, Mrs. Blank and Ronnie to the side. I thought about everything Virgil instructed us to do in the car ride over. 'Plan B' was in full effect. I knew what I had to do. As I rested, I glanced at this wooded area around me. I took it all in….I was okay…for now.

CHAPTER 18

The Chase

I knew I needed to get to the hotel so I could dig up the DVDs that Virgil had left. My intuition was speaking loudly. The agents would be expecting me to go back. I knew there was no way I could go in the actual hotel room to get my stuff. I was going to have to deal with what I had on me. I thought maybe it would be best to go back to the hotel tomorrow instead. That would decrease the chance of them catching me. By tomorrow they would think I'm long gone out of town. I figured it's all about right now... and the rest of today that they're going to search hard for me in Elberton. Plus they knew I'm on foot.

But where could I stay tonight? I thought about a homeless shelter. But even if I went to a homeless shelter, there is no sure thing they would have room for me on short notice. Plus, I don't know where the closest one is and how much money a taxi would cost to get there.

What was the next step? I went over my facts...Virgil advised us not to use and debit or credit cards. I checked my wallet. I had $40 in cash on me. Okay, how far could $40 get me? Let's see, I don't know my way around Elberton, so I would have to call a taxi to get back to the hotel. From there, I would need another taxi to get to the closest train or bus station. And who knows how far that would be! Then of course, I would need enough money to pay for my ticket. And on top of that...Where should I go? How far away from here?

I checked my cell phone. I had almost a full battery. Wait a second...What if my phone is tapped? What if they could trace me from my cell? I had to think faster. I'm only 15 or 20 minutes from the place where the agent had caught Ronnie and I. I got up and started moving.

I came across the backyard of a house and next to it were a few others. It looked as though I was in the back of a suburban type neighborhood, which connected to the woods. A few houses down I saw 2 kids playing in the yard. They looked to be around 7 or 8 years old. At that moment, an idea popped into my head.

I jogged over to the yard where the kids were playing. They luckily did not see me approach as I hid behind the shed in their backyard. I laid down on the ground on the side of the shed and started moaning and groaning. This attracted the kids over to me.

"Who are yooouuuuu?" One kid asked curiously.

"Hey are you okay Mister?" The other one asked.

I continued to moan and groan as if I was in the worst pain of my life.

"Hey kids..." I grunted, "Look, I'm in a lot of pain and I think I need help. Can you go and get your mommy or daddy?" I looked up at them pretending to be in agony. "Please," I insisted.

They ran to the house screaming with their little voices, "Mommy! Mommy!"

It wasn't but a few minutes before the mom came running out.

"Are you okay? What's wrong?" She asked me.

"I'm pretty sure it's my appendix. I've been having trouble with it lately. I was walking on the other side of the woods when it started hurting. There were no houses over there, so I panicked! I ran through the woods to find help. I crawled over to your kids because they were the only people I saw. Please help me."

"Okay," She said, "What's your name?"

"I'm Vince." I grunted.

"Vince can you stand up?" She asked.

"Possibly."

She helped me up and with one arm around her shoulder, we walked slowly to her car. Before I knew it, me, her and her two kids were on our way to the hospital. She was a very nice lady and I really felt bad making all of this up. But I felt I had no choice, this was survival.

She helped me into the emergency room of Elbert Memorial.

"Thank You," I said to her, "You have done a very good deed. I can take it from here, please take your kids home." And out of instinct, I hugged her. It felt really good. Part of me wanted to cry on her shoulder as the feelings of today's events flooded my body.

She left and I went into the waiting room, found a seat and hung out for a few minutes as I thought things through. What better place was there? It was a public place. I can blend in with all the sick and hurt people. It was open all night. It was warm. It had a bathroom. It had a drinking fountain. I could walk to the cafeteria for food. Virgil would have been proud!

I walked over to the cafeteria and I hung out there for a few hours after spending $7 on food. I got some extra fruit for the morning as well. I felt safe around all the people. I considered calling the police, but it was just a thought. Virgil was pretty clear that this agency was bigger than the police and I believed him. I was on my own here.

I took this relaxing time to reflect on everything that happened. I wondered if Ronnie, Virgil and Mrs. Blank were dead. I wondered what the agents plans were to catch me and get this tape. I thought about Virgil's talk in the car and the reality that I would have to leave the Atlanta area for at least a month. What would I do for money? How would I survive? What about school? The year is done in a few weeks...Would they flunk me? And my poor parents, they're going to worry themselves sick. Should I write them a letter like Virgil talked about?

Then my thoughts shifted to Virgil's quick thinking back at Mrs. Blank's. The light went off in his head that the house was bugged when the owl speaking to Ronnie came up. The owl said "It didn't have to be this way." That's the same thing the agent had said when he caught up to Ronnie and I. The thought occurred to me that he knew our last names too. Combine that new knowledge with the fact that Ronnie and Victoria were visited by an agent during the making of the film and it's clear that we have been watched this whole time. My assumption was that they didn't act on it because we were just 'college kids" and they hoped that it wouldn't go far. I guess we crossed their line when we entered that tunnel.

My thought came back to Virgil and how he reacted after that light bulb went off in his head. I can learn from him, on the spot without much thought at all, he wrote that note to me and advised me to get the blank tapes in everyone's pocket. The tapes in the pocket proved to be valuable, as it had allowed me to escape with the footage.

But the biggest question was still on the table. Even if I escape...How would I get this footage out to the world? That's the whole point of all this, isn't it? That's the mission right? How? Do you know? Because I didn't know! I laid my head down on the cafeteria table and actually fell asleep. Go figure, I didn't even need the emergency room.

CHAPTER 19

The Bush

When I awoke, I had that feeling of not knowing where I was for about a minute. Then the cold reality of my situation hit, as I watched people walk by sitting down at their tables for breakfast. It actually wasn't a bad place to blend in and rest. I'm sure others thought I was here overnight as a loved one was in surgery or something.

After I used the bathroom and had some fruit, I called a taxi from a hospital phone. I took some deep breaths to relax myself as the anxiety of not knowing what was going to happen made its way through my body. All I could hope for, was that the agents think I left town already and would not have their eyes on the hotel. Just to be sure, I decided to have the taxi bring me to a local clothing store so I could buy a hoodie sweatshirt and a baseball cap. My thought was that this may help in hiding my identity from someone looking from afar. I knew I didn't have much money left, but it was a risk I felt I had to take.

I had the taxi drop me off at the gas station next to the Days Inn. The cost of my trip came to $16. My new hoodie and cap cost $15. This brought me down to only $9. I figured not getting caught in Elberton was a better investment. I was thinking of calling another taxi, and taking money out of an ATM right as the taxi was waiting for me. That way, I would be on the road by the time they knew my location. I was also thinking of having the taxi take me back to the hospital, in the event the agents tried to intercept me at the train station. One more night to throw them off couldn't hurt. I'm not sure it was the best plan, but it seemed like an okay decision.

With my hood up over my new baseball cap, I slowly walked over to the hotel. My eyes were sharp, I scanned everything like I was a machine. My heart pounded with fear of agents jumping out and getting me, but that fear seemed to make me feel more aware of my surroundings. I observed every parked car, looking for anyone present as I walked towards the back. Nothing looked suspicious.

And there it was, the bush with purple around it. I looked as inconspicuous as I could to my left and right before crouching down. I started digging through the dirt with my hands just as Virgil had suggested. It didn't take long for my fingers to bang into something. It was a shoe box! I dug around it, and shifted the dirt away, finally bringing it to the surface. It had some weight to it! There definitely wasn't just 3 DVDs in there. I went to open it...I paused...then decided to look later. The priority right now was getting off this hotel property. I started making my way down the street and heading towards a McDonald's that I saw on the taxi ride over. I figured I could get a coffee and then sit and go through this shoe box.

I surveyed the McDonald's as I sat in the back with my coffee and box. I didn't see anything suspicious. Although I was disappointed that I stepped foot in the corporate giant that I so adamantly preached others to stay away from. I opened the box slowly. I didn't want to look like a kid on Christmas morning ripping off the wrapping paper to get to the new toy. There were 3 items in the box. There was a brown paper bag, a notebook and the three DVD's that Virgil mentioned. My curiosity was piqued and at that moment I ironically started to feel like the kid on Christmas morning ripping off the wrapping paper to get to the new toy. What was written in the notebook? What's in the paper bag?

I decided to go for the bag first. I slowly opened it up and looked in. I was shocked at what I saw. It was stacks of money! I brought my head back up to view the restaurant to see if anyone was staring at me. It felt like everyone was, but they weren't. I looked back in the bag and couldn't help but smile in relief as there were stacks of one hundred dollar bills. At that moment I felt a tremendous rush of gratitude flush through me. Counting the money at that moment would be a bad idea, but just knowing I had enough to leave town was a relief. All that worry and anxiety of budgeting the $40 of cash I had on me, and not being able to use my credit or debit card was just swept away in an instant.

I opened the notebook.

M or R,

If you're reading this right now, then you had to 'close the store'. The truth is...Life has officially changed for you and is probably over for me.

I knew that coming into this situation. I knew that taking this journey with you guys was going to more than likely result in my demise. I had accepted that before I drove down to meet with you, so please don't feel like you're responsible in any way. This was the fate that I chose. Knowing all of that, I needed to create a solid 'Plan B' for you, so you could carry out the mission. You remember what your mission is right?

I smiled and nodded my head, as if Virgil was sitting next to me and speaking the words out loud.

This notebook is full of useful information for you and your new life. I hope that I can guide you as best as I can so we can carry out our purpose. First thing is first...let's go over the rules of keeping you alive.

1. Never pay for anything with debit, credit or check. Always cash.

2. If you feel the need to write home, you only do it once, and you send the letter to a friend that can hand deliver to your folks.

3. Never log in and or use any of your email or social media accounts.

4. Change your hairstyle ASAP.

5. Wear hats as much as you can.

6. Get a quality book bag that is sturdy enough for you to run with.

7. Create a new identity. Get a new driver's license and passport done. When you meet new people, use a different name every time. Keep in mind, every time you use a new identity, you need to create a short backstory for each one. Where is he from? How old is he? Why is he here? What's he do for work? Etc.

8. Keep your finger on the pulse of the news. Especially in Georgia and on the alternative topic websites. By looking at both, you can decipher truths.

9. Throw your cell phone in the nearest trash can.

10. In the paper bag there is $60,000 Dollars. Spend it very wisely.

11. I recommend picking up a strong spiritual practice. Meditation will help you stay grounded.

12. Never forget your priority. Protect the footage at all cost. You hold the key.

These are my top 12. There is more, but I'm going to assume you can handle them with common sense. But for right now, you need to get out of town! Call a taxi and have them take you to the train station in Toccoa. The agency will be expecting you to leave from the train in Elberton. When you get there, hop a train down to Miami. Once you get to Miami and you're checked into your hotel safely, go to the Sunset Tattoo Parlor on Southwest 72nd St. and ask for a man named Oscar Gutierrez. Tell Oscar that you are interested in taking dance lessons. He will take care of your identity. While you're staying in the hotel for 2-3 Days, look up rooms to rent on Craigslist.com as they will be much cheaper than hotels. Look for something with no lease or commitments.

I want you to stop reading this notebook now. Don't let curiosity cause you to read further. And that includes on the train as well. Focus on the task at hand. The world is depending on you! You have your instructions.

Good luck,

V

I felt so many emotions run through me. I felt relief that I now had a guide. I felt fear for getting caught by the agency. I felt curiosity of what else was in the notebook. I felt grief for having to leave my parents with no explanation. And I felt pain for whatever happened to Ronnie, Virgil, and Mrs. Blank. I finished my coffee and put everything back in the shoe box. I knew I needed that bag ASAP to carry this stuff. I couldn't carry around a shoe box!

I walked outside and threw my cell phone in the trash as instructed. Next to the trash was a newspaper stand with a stack of Elberton Star's. With Virgil's words still in my head, I picked up a paper to take with me. I started to make my way down the street to the nearest gas station in sight. I would call a taxi from there. On my way to Toccoa, I can have them bring me to a store so I can buy a backpack and some underwear and socks. The plan was in motion.

As I walked down the street, I glanced down at the newspaper. The front page headline of the Elberton Star read, *"Conspiracy Theorist Murders a Witch and a Drug Dealer."*

CHAPTER 20

The Story

A man killed a woman and her dog in an Elberton neighborhood before chasing down a college student and shooting him twice, police said. Officers found the suspect and one of the victims in the living room of an Elberton farmhouse. The other victim was found not too far down the street.

The authorities said the suspect used a Glock 9MM Handgun. The suspect is believed to be Virgil Riley, 54, from North Carolina, a reporter for a conspiracy theory website. The woman who was shot once in the head was Barbara Blank, 62, a widowed homemaker who was believed by most of her town to practice the Wiccan religion. She recently made national headlines when she claimed her dog was abducted and then returned with its voice box missing. She has lived in Elberton for two decades and her husband and son both died on the farmhouse property as well.

The other victim was Ronald Simmons, 21, of Decatur, GA. He was a college student who was an apparent marijuana dealer police chief Paul Levesque said. Simmons was found shot twice a half mile up the road and had a quarter pound of marijuana on him, including a marijuana cigarette half smoked by his side.

It is thought that Riley was disturbed by the national story of the witch and her dog, and traveled to Elberton to murder them both.

Simmons may have heard the shootings while he was walking the dirt road outside while smoking. Riley could have noticed Simmons, chased him down and killed him, said the police chief. If that's the case, then Simmons is a victim of being in the wrong place at the wrong time. Riley was found dead on Blank's front lawn from a self-inflicted gun wound to the head. He also had scratches and bruises on his body, which may indicate that he tussled with either Simmons or Blank. The dog was also found dead from a gun wound. An investigation is underway.

I really felt like I was gonna puke. My stomach was in knots and my head was spinning. Traffic whizzed by me as I stood motionless on the sidewalk with the newspaper in my hand. I just couldn't believe what I'd just read. I sat down on the grass to my left. Standing was not a good option at that moment.

The other side completely manipulated everything to create a new story. They painted Ronnie as a drug dealer, Virgil as a nut case, and Mrs. Blank was already a 'witch' in the eyes of many. The media would have everything they needed to solidify it too. Ronnie was a known pothead among friends, family and students in our building. Virgil worked for an alternative topic website and spent half his life researching conspiracies. And Mrs. Blank...Well she had rabbits out back, a dog that couldn't make barking noises, and the deaths of her son and husband. The odds were stacked against the truth.

At that moment, I understood the power of the other side...They could swoop into your life at any given moment and manipulate situations to have you take a left instead of a right so to speak. They could make things happen, and then use those things later on for 'damage control'. It seems as though they would go all out if the situation called for it.

A decade ago or more, they created the story of Mrs. Blank being a witch in Elberton. It now makes sense why they did this. The other side needed their agents to protect that property as best as possible. Not only did making Mrs. Blank a witch keep people away from the farmhouse, but it feeds into the end-game of this story. Most will assume she was murdered because she was a crazy witch and casted a spell on her dog. The agency had that leverage the whole time. A just-in-case 'Plan B', which we had forced them to cash in on.

I'm sure 'Plan A' was to keep people away from that property, so they could continue to do work in the tunnel. Whether they were mining the gold themselves, or they were waiting for the ET's to return, they didn't want anyone near there. It's clear to me now, the agency didn't want Mrs. Blank to die. They didn't even want Ronnie, Virgil or I to die, they just wanted us to go away and mind our own business. They tried to scare Ronnie. They tried to get information from Victoria. They made sure the officer that was snooping was fired. And as for Mrs. Blank's husband and son, they got too close... just as we did over the past few days.

The agency had a good thing going, and they put a lot of work and effort into creating the situation. Truth be told, no one went near the tunnel...until Ronnie and I came around wanting to do a documentary. Instead of doing a documentary on food, 3 people and a dog were dead. And on top of that, I can't go home! Go figure, before I can even legally buy a beer, I'm on the run from a dangerous unknown agency controlled by a shadow government. And there's no doubt that I am public enemy number one to this agency. Not only do I have the footage that would expose everything, but I ruined their contained situation that they put years of hard work into. I wondered what information they had to use against me. How can they manipulate the situation to paint me as the 'bad guy' to the public?

And then it hit me. My roommate, my friend, my partner in this film project... was dead! I thought back to all the recent memories of working on this project. I thought about that moment when he was so adamant about doing the film on Mrs. Blank. It was he who convinced me it was a great story...and now he's gone. I thought about his family. And certainly, if being killed wasn't enough, now he's painted as a drug dealer in the paper. I became overwhelmed with emotion. For the first time since everything happened, I started to cry. My body jerked as I weep violently. Cars flew by, while my pain in the form of tears ran down my face. I felt like a five year old boy, lost at the grocery store just looking for my mommy.

After about 10 minutes, I stood up. I had to focus if I wanted to survive, and I had to focus if I wanted to complete this mission. If I was captured and that footage was destroyed, then Mrs. Blank, Damien, Virgil and Ronnie would have died for nothing! I felt determined to succeed. I had the money, I had the instructions, and most importantly...I had the reason. I kept moving. It's time to get the hell out of Elberton.

CHAPTER 21

The Train

The train station was a nerve-racking experience. All I could do was put the brim of my baseball cap down as far as it could go, and hope that no agents were in the area. I tried my best not to look suspicious or nervous. I either did a good job or no agents were there, because I got onto the train with no problem.

With a long trip ahead of me, I was tempted to open up the notebook and read more. But Virgil insisted that I don't read till I get to the Miami hotel. I'm assuming that his intention was for me to rest. To relax and bring my stress level back down, as the last few days have been the most stressful of my life. I was relieved to be on the train safe and sound, and happy that I scored an empty seat next to me. It didn't take long for me to doze off.

I felt a tapping on my knee and a familiar voice calling my name. I slowly opened my eyes from a deep sleep and instantly jerked up when I saw his face. It was Dr. Hickenbottom!

"Sorry to startle you Mark," He said.

I was in shock. My mouth felt numb. "Whaaa what are you doing here?"

He smiled. "I figured it was important that we had a conversation."

"A conversation? How did you get here man!?"

"Mark...Just relax. First things first. Are you okay? Are you injured or anything?"

"No, I'm fine." I said, still wondering what the hell my college professor was doing next to me on the train to fucking Miami!

He let out a small sigh, then looked out the window. "Well, back in Marietta, people are concerned. Ronnie is dead and you're missing. Of course, you both being roommates, it just looks suspicious you know? It won't be long before they start wondering what your role is in this double homicide."

"Dr. Hickenbottom, I didn't do…."

"I know." He said as he put his hand on my shoulder, "Mark, I know more than you think. That's why I am here."

I felt so utterly confused.

"My understanding is that you have footage of the Guidestones and the tunnel? Is that correct Mark?" He looked at me in a caring manner.

"I...uhhhh...I..."

"Mark, you can trust me okay? I'm not part of the agency. I'm on your side."

"How do you know about the agency?" I asked.

He smirked. "The agency works for the other team...the other side...the bad guys if you will." He looked out the window again as we zipped down the railroad. "I guess I should explain huh?"

He turned his head back to me and looked me in the eye.

"The truth is, I'm not an actual college professor. That's just my cover. I actually work for a group of very important....well...I guess you can say 'beings'. The good guys Mark. The same guys that built those Guidestones to help humanity start over and the same guys that helped speed up the evolution of man. Virgil has told you about the Annunaki I presume?"

"Yes. Briefly. How....How do you know Virgil? Wait? What do you mean you work for them?"

Dr. Hickenbottom smirked again. "Virgil worked with us. He was an insider. A journalist with integrity on getting the truth out to the public. My team who sides with Enki always gave him knowledge and information. We all want the same thing. We all want humans to thrive. To get back to the laws of nature and to live with love and peace. No wars, no animal cruelty, no preservatives in the food, no polluting the air. You get the idea. So, we helped Virgil, and many others along the way."

I shook my head, still in disbelief. "Like who else?" I asked.

"Well, we helped Zecharia Sitchin."

I was confused. "I don't know who that is."

"He was a major part of explaining the Anunnaki & Sumerian tablets to the world. We chose him, and helped him translate the tablets. With being one of the few scholars able to read and interpret ancient Sumerian and Akkadian clay tablets, he based his bestselling books on texts from the ancient civilizations of the near east. Drawing both widespread interest and criticism, his controversial theories on the Anunnaki origins of humanity have been translated into more than 20 languages and featured on radio and television programs around the world. But of course, he was looked at as a nut job, as the other side manipulated the people through the media. They even made a website for him called Sitcheniswrong.com.

I still felt confused…

"We visited Erich Von Daniken as well. I'm assuming you never heard of him either?"

"Never." I replied.

"We got to him in the mid 1960's and asked him to write a book. It was about "ancient astronauts" who visited earth and influenced early human culture. He speaks of the Egyptian pyramids, Easter Island, Moai and Stonehenge all being artifacts from us. He also describes ancient artwork throughout the world as containing depictions of astronauts, air and space vehicles, extraterrestrials, and complex technology.

"You mean like the ones we saw in the Elberton tunnel?"

"Yes. Those artworks were put on those walls many centuries ago. We marked our territory. Are you familiar with David Icke?"

"No." I replied.

"Okay, well we also helped him. We actually spoke to him and chose him to be the guy to expose the other side in these new times. He really took to the mission well. But, it wasn't long before the other side made him look like he was out of his mind also. He's still around though. He does lots of lectures and still writes books. But you'll never see him on CNN. The internet has helped get word out. The people really can do tons of research and come to their own conclusions. We need the internet because the other side controls the mainstream media."

"Is there anyone you guys helped out that I would know? I asked.

"Maybe. Recently about 13 years ago we approached a rap artist named Germaine Williams. He goes by the name Canibus. Have you heard of him?"

"Yes! He used to be on a lot of mix tapes. I know who he is. Never really got deep into his stuff though," I said.

"He put out a song called 'Channel Zero' in 1998 that was pretty in depth. He was on the rise and was about to go into the mainstream. We thought it was a great opportunity and he wanted to help."

"So what happened?" I asked.

"The other side came around and crushed our hopes. They managed to turn the music industry against Germaine by having him get into a quarrel with a legendary artist by the name of LL Cool J. Germaine was basically blackballed from the mainstream. By the time poor Germaine's third album came out, he was considered an 'underground' rap artist who sold a few thousand records instead of millions of records. So...We lost that battle, but he is still making music and he has a core audience. He really puts out a lot of knowledge and does it creatively. He is an amazing Poet. He just put out a project called 'Melatonin Majik' which is a reference to the pineal gland. Do you know of the pineal gland Mr. Calloway?"

"No, I don't."

"Okay, well bottom line is," He paused. "We just need to get the truth out. It's been hidden for so long. We did a lot of work getting all the knowledge into the Library of Alexandria, and the other side came and burned it to the ground by manipulating the people." He looked out the window again and sighed. "Such a shame, there was so much in that library that could have changed the world." He looked back at me. "The other side has continuously had a leg up on us. Until now."

"You're speaking of the footage I have?" I asked.

"Yes." he said. "We must keep you and the footage safe. You are the only human alive who has been inside that tunnel and has the footage to prove it. It's time for the world to know the truth. They need to know that an alien race created intelligent man and taught them how to live in a society. They need to know and practice the laws of nature. They need to know that there is a group that manipulates them to gain power over them. They need to know they are slaves."

I sighed. "This is heavy stuff." I paused, "So, who are you exactly?"

"I am an enlightened watcher. I work for the Enki side of the Anunnaki."

"So, when you go home...Are you Michael Hickenbottom? I'm confused."

"I am him. For now. He's a fake person Mr. Calloway. We created his identity and backstory about 3 years ago. Then we implanted him into the system. I walked into the University and got hired just as any credible professor would. I was trained to teach filmmaking.

I actually enjoy it to be honest," Hickenbottom chuckled.

"It's very similar to undercover police work. My mission was to guide you Mark. My supervisors planted me at the school to help motivate you to do this documentary. Ronnie was manipulated to suggest Mrs. Blank to you...and so on and so forth."

"Wow!" I was stunned. "So the good side manipulates too?"

"Yes. We have no other choice. You and all humans have free will. Remember I mentioned that to you before? I or anyone else can't make you do anything. We can only manipulate to get the result that we need. Every now and again, we actually come talk to someone, as I told you about earlier."

"So, I'm in the same category as Sitchin, Icke and.....whatever the other guy's name was?"

"Yes. But you must be trained to use the natural energy source and your pineal gland."

"What's the pineal?" I asked.

"It's commonly referred to as the third eye. It's an endocrine gland in your head that does many things, including help you dream. It's a very powerful tool, this is how one would communicate through telepathy. Most human pineals are calcified by the time they're 12 years old. You see, the other side manipulated America, by getting the food corporations to get people hooked on unnatural artificial foods. Between that and the fluoride in the water, the average American has no direct spiritual connection to the universe."

"What about religious people?" I asked.

"Religion is exactly what the other side wants. It's traditional programming. Those that follow a religion are stuck in the box of belief. While many become better citizens strictly following their religion, they are not capable of using their God-given powers. But it's worth noting, neither are Atheists. They also are stuck in the box of belief. You see, it's because they both adamantly believe in something that they have no experience on. Only stories, traditions, and assumptions. It's those that leave the box of belief and learn to use their pineals that become god-like. When you become enlightened or god-like, you can then tap into the natural energy source and be able to see and do things you never imagined. It's the difference between the guy that reads a ton of books on fixing a car, versus the guy that actually fixes the car. Experience is needed to know. You must know because you do, not because you were told."

"So…" I paused in thought, "The other side doesn't want humans to become spiritual beings and discover their true powers?"

"That's correct. The world hasn't had a Buddha or Jesus type figure on earth in a while right? I mean, there have been a few Yogi's along the way that made an impact, but their knowledge didn't spread as wide. You see, they were enlightened beings and tried to teach it to people, but the other side was too strong. Now, enlightenment is almost extinct on earth due to the other side's manipulation. It took some time, but they eventually started to master how to keep people as sheep. Think about this…You can't herd cats, right? They're too independent. So it's necessary to keep humans as obedient sheep to avoid a spread of enlightenment. They do this through classical conditioning and strategic programing. It's actually not that hard, especially now with technology. Television has become the ultimate tool to program the people and dictate what people love, hate, eat, wear, and believe in. The other side did massive experiments, many of which still exist today.

"Experiments?" I was confused. "Like what?"

Hickenbottom smirked. "Well, let's see….Cake for birthdays, Santa

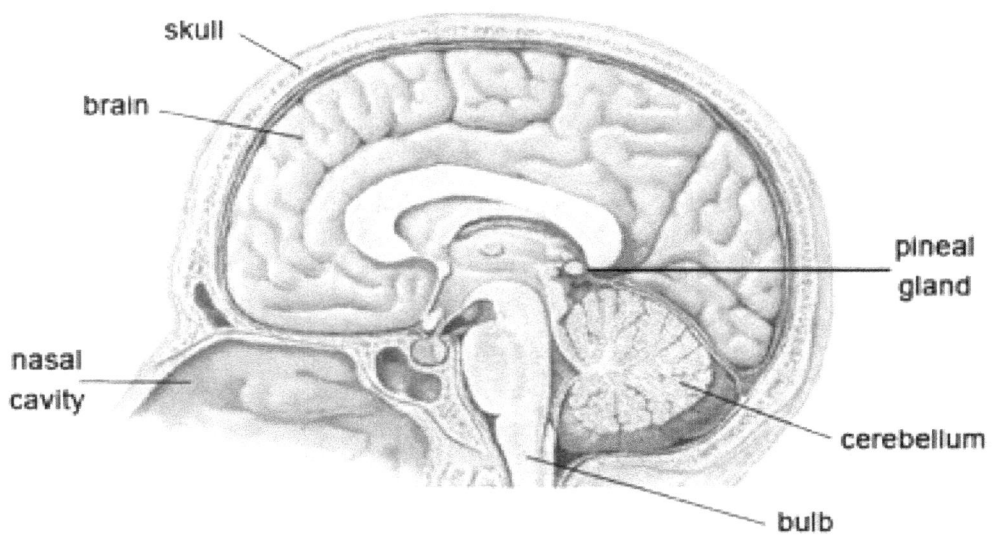

at Christmas, fancy jewelry and expensive cars in mainstream rap music, the fear of terrorism, the concept of marriage and weddings, pornography,

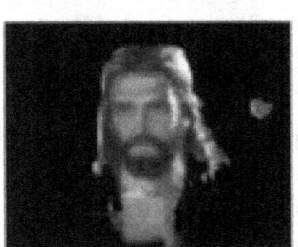

Matthew 6:22 If your eye be single, your whole body shall be full of light.

pizza and chicken wings on football Sundays, women wearing make-up and getting boob jobs, drug dealing and gun use in the lower income neighborhoods. Mark, I could go on with this. These were all experiments of programming. And it all worked. Especially the concept of money. That's the biggest manipulation on the planet. It's the end-all-be-all for the sheep. Money is worshipped and money is depended upon. It's the backbone of human society."

"Wow." I said. "I always wondered why we ate cake to celebrate birthdays...like...Why not apples or beans? I'm assuming bacon and eggs as breakfast foods is a manipulation too?!

"Oh. Indeed." Hickenbottom continued, "In fact, food is a major weapon. Besides man's original food which was fruits, vegetables, nuts, seeds, sprouts and herbs, humans have become addicted to animal flesh, animal fluids, cooked oils, refined sugars, wheats, and more. You see, these foods congest the human lymphatic system, create mucus, and cause sickness. Now, after sickness comes what Mark?"

"Medicine!" I blurted out.

"That's right. So this is how they get people on the prescription drugs and start creating even better behaved sheep that are weak and fragile."

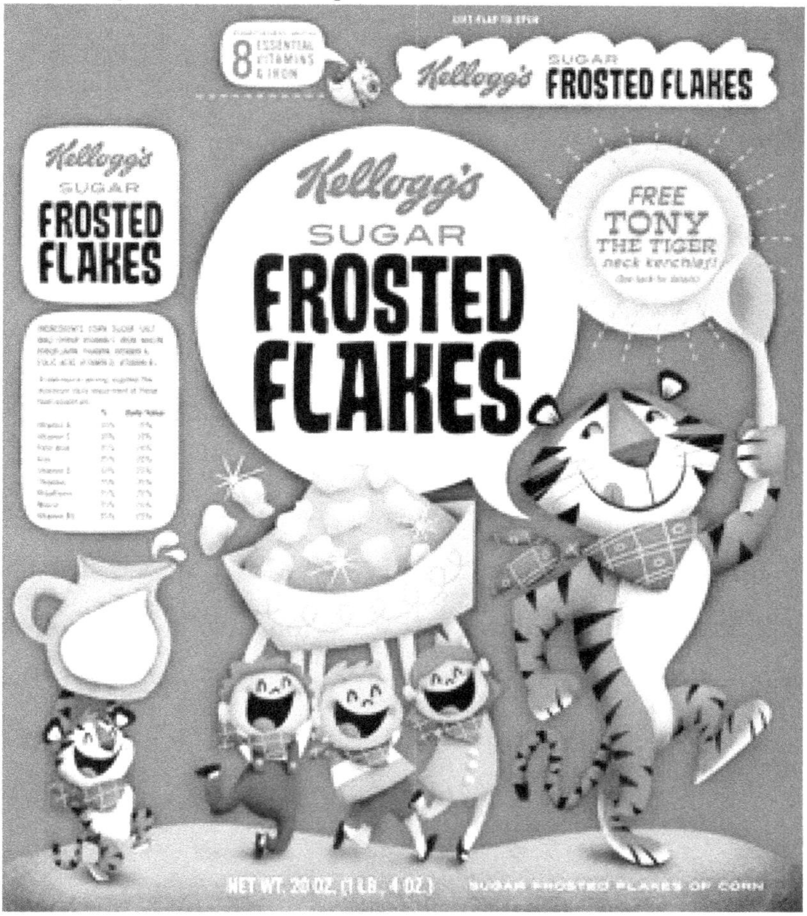
8 ESSENTIAL VITAMINS & IRON
Kellogg's SUGAR FROSTED FLAKES
Kellogg's SUGAR FROSTED FLAKES
Kellogg's SUGAR FROSTED FLAKES
FREE TONY THE TIGER neck kerchief!
NET WT. 20 OZ. (1 LB., 4 OZ.)
SUGAR FROSTED FLAKES OF CORN

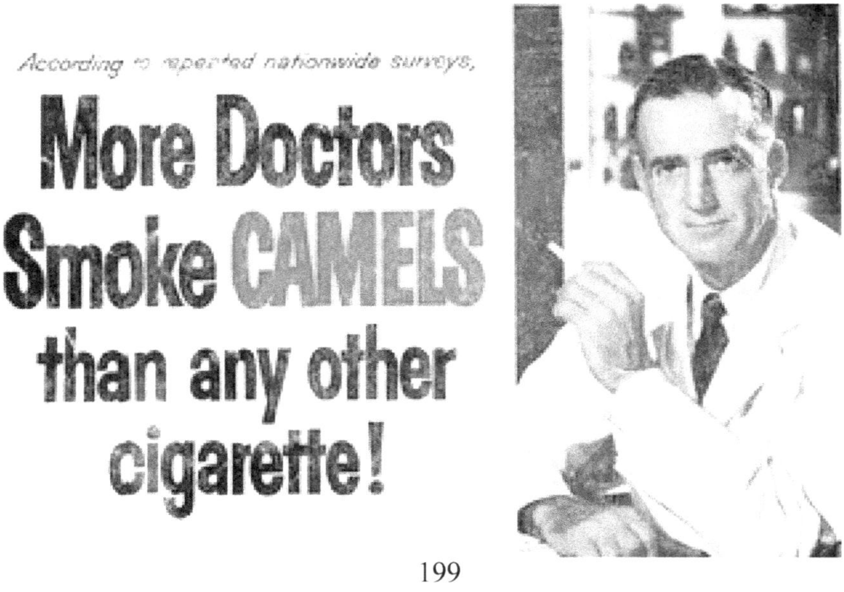
More Doctors
Smoke CAMELS
than any other
cigarette!

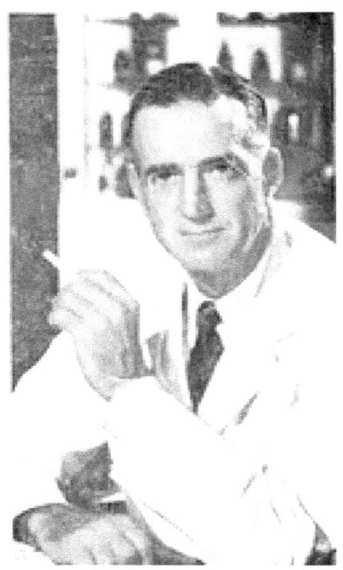

I was feeling a little angry now. "And I always wondered why women wear make-up. They've been taught to always improve their looks to be beautiful. You're right, it's all a manipulation of free will. That's fucked up man."

Hickenbottom continued as I sat in awe. "You see, there's only an illusion of freedom Mark. That illusion is granted by the perception of having choice. You have the choice between all sorts of different jobs and careers, but you have to work to live right? You have the choice between all sorts of television shows, but you still see the commercials don't you? You have the choice between many different colleges, but they all cost a pretty penny don't they? You have the choice between many fast food restaurants, but they're all bad for your health aren't they? Do you understand?"

"Yes, I get it." I replied. "My goodness, all we have to do is walk down a grocery store aisle and see all the choices of fake, artificial, food with chemicals in it. Shit! The cereal aisle alone with all the colorful boxes to attract kids! The illusion of fucking choice! It all keeps the pineal gland suppressed and creates weakness. Damn."

Hickenbottom shook his head as he seemed satisfied that it was all making sense to me.

I took a deep breath. Then another question crossed my mind. "Okay, so I gotta ask, where does the tunnel come into all this?"

"As you know the Anunnaki need gold. Monatomic gold is an important part of their culture and their world. Gold is great at superconductivity. Gold is also important to humans, it's just humans have been programmed to use it as money. Well, Elberton just happens to have an abundance of it underground. This is why we put the Guidestones there. When it was time to start over, humans would have the monument to guide them, and the gold to enhance them."

I was confused. "But why gold...if it's not of monetary value to them?"

"Food. The Anunnaki fed on mostly golden naan bread and grapes. Grapes in general are one of, if not the most powerful foods in the world. They have amazing properties that keep your lymphatic system moving flawlessly while removing mucus from the body. Especially the concords. This process of eating grapes and drinking wine would essentially boost your immune system to epic proportions. But the bread was special. It was made from a white powder from burned gold. This golden naan bread helped the Anunnaki themselves become more intelligent and enlightened. Of course, humans having the same bloodline, it worked on them too."

He had my undivided attention. "Isn't there supplements out there with gold in it?"

"Yes. It's called Ormus. It was discovered in 1975 by an Arizona farmer named David Hudson. He found an unusual element in his soil and laid it out to dry in the hot sun. Eventually, it burnt up and exploded in a flash of light which made it disappear. But when he dried it without using the sunlight...It powderized.

I was intrigued. "How could it have disappeared? Where did it go? It vaporized?"

"It went to another dimension. We have many realms. This is how humans think they see ghosts. Anyway, I'm sure Virgil will teach you all of this. But getting the gold to go to another dimension...This is what happened to Moses."

"Moses? What about him?" I asked.

"Well, the burning bush was actually gold. When you burn the gold at 70 Seconds or so at sun temperature it produces a powder just like Hudson discovered. During the process there is some steam you can inhale. Moses was able to take it in and tap into another dimension where he was able to speak to Anu, the Anunnaki leader at the time. He was then given the 10 Commandments to share with the public. It was supposed to help humans. Of course, many didn't and still don't follow them. Look at 'Thou Shalt Not Kill'. We have religious people who eat animals every day. Well, those animals needed to be killed right? And humans don't just kill them, they torture them in factory farms. See, they interpreted it as 'Thou Shalt Not Kill...Humans."

I got excited. "That's what I was telling people when I went Vegan last year!"

"Yes. You were waking up Mark. Now, back to the ark of the coveted. It was actually an electronic machine that helped heat up the gold to make it into a powder. Of course, this technology is way ahead of its time back then. The other side, stole it and hid it. They don't want humans to consume gold. This would open their pineals and strengthen their brain tissues."

"Wow." I said. I was amazed at what I was hearing. "That explains the golden calf story too! So this gold is more useful than just buying stuff? I know we have electricity in our bodies, right?"

He grinned. "Yes. Our brains receive messages by electronic impulses which travel through a white substance that's in our brain. Well, gold just happens to be the best conductor of electricity. Humans vibrate at frequencies. We have a nervous system. We tend to increase those frequencies when we eat lots of fruits. If you add gold into the mix, humans would become enlightened pretty fast. Of course the other side frowned on it. They always viewed humans as pets or slaves. In fact, the last known person to eat this golden bread at a high level was the second Pharaoh of Egypt. But you...You will too, Mark."

"I will?" I asked.

"Yes. Virgil will guide you. He left you a notebook correct?"

I nodded my head yes.

"Okay, one of the tasks in there will be to increase your vibrational energy by consuming this gold. For now, be conscious of eating lots of fruits and practicing meditation. You have to start detoxing your body and removing all the wastes as well as strengthening your mind. You will need to be strong mentally and physically so you can survive. There's a storm coming."

My mind instantly went to what Virgil was talking about with HAARP. "Wait. Which side has control over HAARP?" I asked anxiously.

Hickenbottom smirked. "We do Mark, we do."

"Holy Shit." I began to panic. "So, the Enki side, your side, created HAARP and the Guidestones? So.... You're planning something of biblical proportions?"

Hickenbottom gazed back out of the train window. "Yes Mr. Calloway, and you're the human that's going to create the human revolution. Someone needs to."

"You mean, the new world order? I became more anxious. "Dr. Hickenbottom, you want me to be involved with killing people with this weather machine and…."

He cut me off. "Mr. Calloway, the other side's goal is to enslave humanity. Over the next decade you will see more manipulated hate and terrorist crimes on mainstream media which will lead to a major gun control ruling. That means humans will be unarmed and vulnerable. The other side will then have complete control of their sheep. They will then continue to manipulate humans to be money-hungry, sick, and fearful, all while multiplying till the population gets up to 10 billion. 10 billion obedient slaves I might add, that can be manipulated and be put to work either digging for gold or fighting as part of their intergalactic army. Does that sound appealing to you when you're 50 years old Mr. Calloway?"

I shook my head. "No."

He continued, "We on the other hand, we want to enlighten humans and create a heaven on earth. But we can't do that unless we follow the laws of the Guidestones. That includes an incredible sacrifice to decrease the population to 500 million people. And these can't be any 500 million people. No, we need the healthy, young, and open minded people so we can nurture their potential to become enlightened beings. And then, we can leave and let humans thrive. Now, how does that world sound when you're 50?"

"It sounds better. Yes." I replied as my voice shook.

"We believe in you Mr. Calloway. You are the prototype. You will soon become enlightened and then you will see what humans are capable of. And then, then you will see what your world can be like. We just need to keep you and the footage safe. The other side is coming for you. Virgil will tell you what to do next. My job here is done."

I jerked up out of my seat... Hickenbottom was gone!

The man in front of me turned around. "Hey kid, you alright?

"Yeah...Why?" I rubbed my eyes, still feeling in a daze.

"You were having a dream or something back there...Talking about Moses and a burning bush..."

CHAPTER 22

The City

Even with the massive amounts of stress that I was under, I could still feel the amazement of Miami. After the taxi dropped me off at the hotel, I walked around in awe of this paradise. The tropical weather made my skin feel like it was shining. The beautiful women walked by in all assortments of colors and shapes making my mind dance. I could smell all sorts of cuisines floating through the air making my taste buds jump. I had the feeling of being on vacation. But I wasn't. My mind shifted right back to the situation I was involved with. My eyes scoured around the area, wondering who was part of the other side. I could trust no one.

After checking into my room, I decided to grab something to eat at an Indian restaurant across the street. I always appreciated Indian cuisine because they had great meatless options. I walked in and was greeted by a very friendly Indian man as he sat me over to the left side of the buffet. The vibe was great. Some light Indian music, great smells from the food, and a packed room. The waiter poured me some water and instructed me to enjoy the buffet whenever I was ready. Just as I got up and took a step over to the plethora of food, I heard a light voice call my name. I could not believe what I saw when I turned around. It was Victoria!

"It's so good to see you!" She said with a big smile as she stood a few feet in front of me.

I was stunned. So many emotions ran through me. I was excited to see this woman who I was so attracted to, yet scared to death of why she was there? Did she follow me? Is she on the other side? Was she an Anunnaki?

"Victoria…" I paused and sat back down and invited her to do the same. She looked so concerned.

"What are you doing here?" I asked.

She shot me an innocent smile. "Well, I know it's going to sound strange...but I was told to come here.

"What….? By who? Are you following me Victoria? No one knows that I'm here!"

"No...No...Not at all. I know this is creepy, but it's just so hard to explain." She paused as she looked down at the table.

"A man came to me in dream. He told me it was important that I come to Miami on this specific date and find you at this restaurant. I've been here all day. I honestly didn't believe it until you walked in!"

"Wait…" I shook my head in shock. "You're here because of a dream?" My mind raced…and then it dawned on me.

"Wait…Was it a tall gentleman with grey hair and a booming deep voice?"

"Yes!" She replied. "His name was Michael."

"Yep, that's Dr. Hickenbottom." I couldn't believe what I was hearing.

"You know him?" She asked

"Yes, he is… or was my filmmaker professor in college. What else did he say Victoria?"

"I don't think here is the best place. Why don't you eat and then we'll go back to your hotel room and talk. I already ate.

I was hesitant…but very hungry. I agreed.

She flashed that great smile at me again. "The food is pretty spicy. It was my first time having Indian."

I closed the room door behind us. Finally, I would get my

explanation. Victoria sat on the edge of the bed. I sat on at the desk chair. I was eager for answers and still a bit paranoid.

"Before we get into Michael, can you tell me what the news is back in Elberton?"

"It's not good. Everyone is talking about Mrs. Blank like she was evil. It's just so sad, because I could feel that she wasn't."

"No...She wasn't." I replied, "She seemed like a great person that had been through a lot."

"Some are even saying that the conspiracy guy did what needed to be done."

"So Virgil is the bad guy?"

"Yes. Did you know him?" She asked

"Yeah. He is the reason I'm here in Miami right now, and the reason why I'm alive. He was a great guy with a huge heart. He's a hero."

"Oh that is horrible. So how did all this happen?"

"Well, the short story...We made some big discoveries on camera, Virgil came in and guided us, and the bad guys busted in to get the tapes. My friend, Ronnie and I escaped."

I paused, making sure I didn't choke up, "And he got shot as we were fleeing on foot. I made it. He did not. I'm the only survivor."

"Oh honey, I'm so sorry." She frowned.

"Yeah...me too." I said. "Anyway...Any mention of me out that way?"

"There is a report that you're missing, but nothing has been linked or anything." She said.

"Yeah, it's a matter of time before they link it to me and paint me as a villain in the media."

"Who is 'they'?" She asked.

"Virgil and Michael refer to them as 'the other side'. It's really such a long story Victoria. It's like something you would see on the Sci-Fi Channel. You know?"

"Yes, I understand. You don't have to tell me."

"Thanks. So, tell me about Michael visiting you."

"Okay, well, he showed up in a dream a few weeks ago. He introduced himself and explained that he was one of the good guys. He told me that he had an important mission for me and he would show up at a later date to give me my assignment. I didn't think much of it. It was just a quick little dream. Before he left, I asked him if he was an angel....He smiled and said yes."

"Did this happen before or after we interviewed you for the documentary?"

"Oh it was after." She looked to be recalling her thoughts.

"Yeah, not long after actually. Anyway, obviously weeks went by. I got my notorious visit from the FBI guy and then ran back into you at the diner."

I interrupted. "Yes. That was sad day for me. I was looking forward to seeing you again, and wasn't expecting for you to tell me I had to leave. Ya know?"

"Oh I know honey. I didn't want to. I really didn't. You seem so sweet and you're so adorable...but I was paranoid. I just had to do what I had to do."

"I understand." I replied with a smile just realizing she called me sweet and adorable. "Believe me, knowing what I know now, it makes sense. Please continue."

"Okay. Well, he came back two days ago. But this time it wasn't quick. We had what felt like a super long conversation. It didn't feel like a dream at all."

"Yeah he is good at that," I said with a chuckle.

"So he has visited you before too Mark?"

I shook my head yes.

"Oh, that makes me not feel as crazy as I thought I was then!" She patted my knee and smiled.

"So...Tell me more." I said.

"Well, he told me that he had the very important job to help guide you in the right direction. He said that you're in trouble and I need to be your insurance policy."

"My insurance policy? How so?"

"Yes, he said you had a DVD for me to take back home."

I couldn't help but crack a mischievous smile as all the pieces starting making up the puzzle.

"He also said you had a mini DV tape that you would be making a copy of and giving to me to take along with the DVD. I don't even know what a mini DV tape is, but that's what he said. Do you have one of those?"

"Yes." I replied.

"Well, I guess this is pretty real then, huh?" She smiled. "He told me I would find you today or tomorrow at Raja's Indian Cuisine."

"But how would he know I would go there?" I asked.

"He said that was the closest Indian place near the hotel. He informed me that you don't eat meat and he knows you have a taste for Indian food. He expected you to go there for food. I was instructed to stay there all day if I had to. When you walked in, I had already been there for a good 5 hours. The staff must think I'm nuts. After I ate, I just played on my phone to kill the time. Of course I had thoughts that I was following this path for no reason. And it was just a dream. But when you came walking in...It felt so...real."

"Yeah well you scared the shit out of me!" We both busted out in laughter.

"Yeah. I'm sorry. I'm a very spiritual person and I just couldn't ignore Michael's words in the dream. He told me how valuable this footage was, and that the copies needed to be spread out so they're not all in your hands. He said if the wrong people got ahold of the footage, that they would destroy it. He also told me that I would need to protect myself. So he said that I would take a trip with you here in Miami. Something about dancing...?"

"Dancing?" I paused and thought about it. "Ohhhhhhh. Yes I know what he means. I'm supposed to visit a tattoo parlor tomorrow and there I will find a guy that is going to change my identity. I guess you're meant to do the same, huh?"

"I guess so. I don't have much money on me, he said that you would take care of it."

"Yes." I said. "That's not a problem. What did he say to do with your footage?"

"He said when I come back to Elberton, to put the DVD and the tape into a shoe box and bury it next to a bush in the back of the diner and put a purple ribbon around the bottom of the bush."

I smiled. "That's interesting. So...How long did he say for you to stay here?"

"He said to get the footage from you, go to the dancing place, and fly back. He stressed the importance of not being around you too long as you can't be distracted. He was very adamant about you needing to be alone. Anyway...I got on a plane right away. I must admit, I also wanted to be able to see you again."

"Oh yeah?" I cracked a huge grin.

"Yeah." She did the same.

I gazed into her eyes and it was like watching diamonds shine. She put her hand back on my knee.

"Mark, I have to tell you. I feel connected to you. Our energies mesh really well."

I shook my head. "I agree" I said.

She leaned in...and our lips became one. I put my hand on her cheek as she rubbed my thigh. She pulled away from me and gazed into my eyes with an intense stare of passion.

"I want to stay with you tonight," She said.

"Were you told to?" I asked softly.

She slowly moved her petite frame over to mine as she straddled me on the chair and looked into my eyes at close range.

"No." She said. She started kissing me intensely.

CHAPTER 23

The Instructions

Victoria slept in the bed naked with only half the covers on her. I was sitting over on the chair gazing at her, taking her in as I held Virgil's notebook in my hand. She was more gorgeous than Miami! What an unexpected night. It was the most passionate I had ever felt with a woman before. I don't know if it was because she was a few years older than me or if we just had some sort of connection, but it was magic. I felt love.

I opened the notebook to see what my next instructions were.

If you're following the instructions correctly, you should be in the hotel in Miami right now. And there might even be or was an encounter with a certain 'friend'. Listen to this friend, as she has more instructions for you. Remember, no matter what happens in the next day or two, she must leave you. You cannot do this mission unless you are alone. Pay for her travel and store these moments in your memory. Let's continue...

How many times have we seen TV shows and documentaries on aliens? It's presented as subjective, not truth. But they're produced, because they bring in ratings. For ages, ET's have been stereotyped as little green people, like they're characters that your child can be for Halloween. Fictional fantasy that only a small demographic actually believes. And when they do speak up and believe, they are ridiculed as 'crazy'. This is how it has all been set up.

There is much truth in 'fictional' works. The Matrix opened our eyes to living in a programmed world. Star Wars explored the good and bad of enlightened beings. Terminator showed us how man-made machines can take over if we're not careful. And the list goes on. These movies grossed billions and became phenomenon, yet the average person views them as science fiction. If they were presented as truth, they wouldn't have made it to our screens.

Also, the documentary game is in full swing. Films such as 'Loose Change', 'Zeitgeist', etc. are making an impact and slowly getting around to the public. They will never make it to TV. The other side views it as 'underground' so they let it pass. The other side only cracks down on truth that makes it to the mainstream. It is Joe Blow who watches the five o'clock news that they care about. The sheep.

I tell you all of this, because the 'Elberton Enigma' must be handled correctly. If you simply send your footage to CNN, Fox

News or even your local stations...It would not see air time. It won't even be mentioned, as it would get intercepted by the other side. If you put the footage on YouTube, you may get a day or two out of it, but it would be intercepted by the other side and deleted. Even a movie, can get intercepted if it's going through a big movie studio with a big budget.

After much thought, and talks with my consultants, it has been suggested that this story becomes a book. Books fly under the radar more than TV, movies and even documentaries. The other side doesn't intercept books anymore because they think that most people don't like to read. Look at books like the '12th Planet', 'The Celestine Prophecy', and 'The Tigers Fang'. These are just a few, but think about all the books about God, religion, reincarnation, soul traveling, witchcraft, aliens, conspiracies etc. This is our path.

The 'Elberton Enigma' needs to come out as a book! It will be your journal of what happened from the very beginning. This is your chronicle. While it will be presented as fiction, there is a demographic that will understand it. With enough buzz, this book can become a movie, and you already have the footage! Yes, they will perceive it as a 'mockumentary' in the same vein as 'The Blair

Witch Project' or 'Cloverfield'... but this is the only logical way to get it out there Mark! This will create positive and truthful programing until our friend and his crew pulls the trigger on their "storm."

While in Miami, you have three important assignments.

1. To not get caught by the other side.

2. To get your identity changed.

3. To write a book!

This book will need to be written before you set out on your journey because you will have to focus on keeping the footage and yourself safe. It may sound overwhelming, but just start at the beginning from the time you wanted to do this documentary and go all the way till now, in Miami. Don't worry about being the next Stephen King, just do the best you can. Obviously, you will not be able to use real names. Everyone (and their families) needs to be protected. Your story needs to be read so that when it's time for you to speak, you will be heard.

I realize you may not have a computer handy as you're on the run. Go to the library, set up a brand new Gmail account and use their g-drive feature. This will allow you to have your document anywhere you have access to the internet.

Find a cheap room on Craigslist and stay in there as much as you can. Go back and forth to the library and the market for food, and that's it. Do not go sightseeing in Miami. No clubs, no restaurants, no movies, nothing. The more you can stay inside, the better. You're on a mission, not a vacation.

On your way to go see Oscar, make sure you find a production house in town and get a few copies of the DV tape as well. The next time you open this notebook should be when you're done with the book and you have met with Oscar. Nobody can know where you go next. Do NOT tell anyone what your plans are. Trust no one but me and Hickenbottom.

Good Luck,

V

I don't know what I was more floored at when I read this. The fact that I had to write a book about this awful experience, or the fact that Virgil just mentioned Dr. Hickenbottom! It completely creeped me out. Yet, I felt safe. I wondered if Virgil specifically insisted I didn't read the notebook on the train knowing that I would fall asleep, so that Hickenbottom could visit me.

Victoria started moving. She opened her eyes and cracked a smile at me. I couldn't help but grin.

"Well hello there, Superman," She said softly.

"Good morning beautiful lady," I replied shooting a warming smile back at her.

I went over to the bed and kissed her on her forehead and laid down with her. She laid her head on my chest. It felt so perfect.

"We have an exciting day ahead of us huh?" I said.

"I know right? Can't we just stay in all day and commit sins with each other?"

I chuckled. "I wish." I begin to feel a rush of seriousness come over me. I slipped out from under her head, put my hand on her face and kissed her lips.

"Victoria, we have to book your flight for tonight and it makes me feel so sad. You're so awesome. I...I could stay in this bed with you forever."

She started to tear up. "I would love to stay with you Mark." She kissed me and rubbed my face right back.

After another round of lovemaking, some breakfast, booking her flight and one amazing shower, we were out the door. We found a production house and had the mini DV tape duplicated. Then, we were off to see Oscar at the Tattoo parlor.

Chapter 24

The Dance

"Can I help you guys?" The lady at the front desk asked. She had long black hair with tattoos up and down her arm.

"Yes," I replied, "We're here to see Oscar."

She paused. "There's no Oscar here."

"Ummm....Oscar Gutierrez?"

She shook her head. "Nope. But we're running a special on tattoos for the spring if you're interested."

Victoria looked at me signaling that we should leave. But I couldn't give up. This was my mission.

"Listen, I was told to come here to see Oscar, so I could sign up for dancing lessons."

Victoria looked at me like I was nuts. Of course she didn't know the code phrase.

The lady at the front desk paused for a while and looked us up and down.

"Why don't you have a seat? I'll be right back."

About 10 Minutes later, she came back with this tall guy. He was huge. He had to be around 6'6" or so and his arms, chest and face were covered in tattoos.

"So you guys are here for Oscar?"

"Yes." I replied. "For dance lessons."

"Follow me." He instructed.

We followed him towards the back. It was amazing all the artwork we saw on people's bodies as we walked through the shop.

"I'm not sure I would ever be brave enough to get one." I whispered to Victoria as we walked.

She smiled at me. "You saw the only one I have last night."

"I sure did," I said as I grinned.

In the back of the building there was a rusted door. The tall guy opened it, and signaled us to walk through. As the door closed behind us we were greeted by a guy in a luchador mask. He was short, probably about 5'2" or 5'3".

"Who are you? And who sent you?" He said with a Mexican accent.

"I'm Mark and this is Victoria, we came down from Georgia per the instructions of Virgil Riley."

Of course we couldn't see any face expressions with his mask on.

"Okay," He said. Then he nodded his head to the tall guy. "Check them out Chavo."

The tall guy then positioned himself in front of us.

"I need you to turn around and put your hands on the wall. I'm going to pat you both down."

It wasn't a pleasant experience. He checked everything! And I sure didn't like Victoria getting the same treatment. But I guess they had to be safe.

"Coast is clear boss." He said to the masked man.

"We needed to make sure you weren't wearing any wires or had any bugs on you." He said.

"In the business we're in, you never know when the other side is lurking."

"You know about the other side?" I asked naively.

"Do I know about the other side? I could tell you stories that would peel the hair off your arm kid," He chuckled, "Okay, let's take them down Chavo."

Chavo whipped out two pieces of cloth. "I must blindfold you." He said in poor English.

We didn't walk very far. Maybe 20 or so feet before we ended up in some sort elevator that was clearly going down. It was an eerie feeling not being able to see. Not to mention putting complete trust in strangers. Victoria and I held hands. Of course my hands were clammy, and hers felt as smooth as they did the night before.

I couldn't believe what I saw when our blindfolds were taken off. We were in some sort of cave and lodged into the walls were gold! Oscar asked us to have a seat. He had set up a small office. There was a desk, a couch, and a few machines that I couldn't make out. One of them looked like a photo booth.

"Where are we?" Victoria asked.

"Throughout the world there are tunnels and caves where the Anunnaki dug for gold, essay. Some cities have more gold than others, but almost every city has these underground tunnels. We found this one back in 1985. It wasn't occupied so I decided to occupy it."

"Is it monoatomic gold? Are you able to make bread? I asked curiously.

Oscar chuckled. "I see you have received a few lessons. That's good. But yes, this machine right here actually…" He pointed at it. "It heats the gold perfectly to create the powder we need."

"How were you able to build it? It must have taken a while to get it perfect? Are there any others in the world like it?"

"The watchers that I work for instructed me how to make it. It took only about a week to make. Yes, there are others in the world. Not many though. It's privileged information and technology."

"Do you consume the gold yourself?" I asked.

"Yes I do. Every day, essay."

"So...you're enlightened?"

"Yes, you can say that. I have powers if you will."

"Powers?" Victoria asked. Of course she didn't know as much as me, so she must have felt like she was in a movie or something.

"Yes chica, I know how to use my pineal gland. I know how to leave my body and I know how to travel to different dimensions."

"Leave the body? Wait... Can you show up in people's dreams?"

"Yes I can. This is how you would communicate with the average person if you needed to." Oscar said.

I looked at Victoria and she looked stunned. I think it dawned on both of us that this is how Dr. Hickenbottom was able to visit us.

"And you know telepathy I'm assuming?" I asked.

He nodded his head yes. "I can only communicate with others like me."

"So, why the mask Oscar?" Victoria asked.

"I like to play it as safe as I can. I'm a wanted man you must understand. The other side has been looking for me for years. I have Chavo here to help protect me and our cave, but not being seen is a must for me. I help many people. The watchers send who they feel is ready to see me. I was told that you would be coming here Mark."

"By who?" I asked.

"By Senior Hickenbottom."

"Okay, and you know Virgil?"

"Yes, he was a friend and a good guy who fought for the cause." He paused. "Look, I know you have questions, but we don't have much time. Let's get to work. Si?"

I agreed.

They proceeded to take head shots in the camera booth of both me and Victoria. Oscar punched away at the computer and before you knew it, we had new identities. I was handed two passports and two driver's licenses. Victoria was handed one.

"Why do I have two?" I asked him.

"Because you are going on a journey. You may need to switch it up right? Your chica friend here, she only needs one. And really, that one is just in case."

"Just in case what?" Victoria asked in frightened tone.

"Just in case they link you to Mark and you have to run." He said.

I looked at Victoria. I felt horrible. She was in danger because of me? I held her hand. She looked back with a look of warmth.

"Now we have more work to do Senior Mark." Oscar said.

"Like what?" I asked.

"It's time we start your process of enlightenment."

I was shocked. "I'm going to be enlightened? Is it a long process? What do I have to do?" I felt like a kid asking a ton of questions before driving for the first time or something.

"Si essay, I was told to start the process on you. And si, it is a long process, but I can start you off. Mark, how tall are you?"

"I am 5'9"." I replied.

"That is perfect."

"Why is that perfect?"

"We have a gland in our heads called the pituitary. You may remember it from high school anatomy class."

"Yes, I remember it. It's the governor of the glands or something right?"

"Close essay. It is the president. CEO if you will. It controls all the other endocrine glands. The reason I ask your height is because it also controls growth. 5'9" is a great height for a man. If you were short like me, we would know that your pituitary is weak."

"So how did it affect you?" I asked.

"It took me longer to become enlightened because of it."

Victoria chimed in. "So what about if you're tall like he is?" She pointed at Chavo.

"Same thing Señorita. If you are very tall...You probably have an overactive pituitary. This includes all the tall chicos you see on the basketball courts. But Chavo here, he is different. He is of a high bloodline. He was conceived by an earth woman and a watcher. When he became old enough, they trained him and then sent him to protect me and my work. We tattooed his body so he would fit in with our tattoo shop."

"So…Chavo's an undercover Demigod?" I asked him.

"That's one way to put it, si, kind of like Jesus," Oscar said.

"Similar to Jesus...? Was Jesus a Demigod?" Victoria asked.

"That is a good question Señorita", Oscar said. "But we seem to be getting off topic though. Let's get back to the pituitary gland. Mark, your height is a good sign that this process shouldn't take as long as others. As long as you do what you're supposed to of course."

"Okay, what do I have to do?" I asked.

"For one. You must change your diet. High fruits are important. Fruit vibrate at higher frequencies than any other foods. They also clean you out. It is important that you are cleaned out so your body is not full of waste, plaque and toxins."

"I'm Vegan so I eat pretty good," I said.

"Vegan does not mean anything Chico. While it's good that you do not eat meat or dairy, Vegans often consume too many starches or junk foods."

"Yeah...I'm guilty of that," I replied with a smirk.

"Yes, you must cut them out and become pure. Cereals, grains, pastas, and even potatoes should be eliminated. It's all about the fruits and of course the dark grapes."

"What about veggies?" Victoria asked. "We all grew up being told to eat our vegetables."

"Vegetables should be consumed, but understand...They do not vibrate at such high frequencies as fruit and they do not clean like fruit. Stick with leafy greens like spinach, kale, and chard. They are what gives strength and balance," He said.

"Like Popeye." I said with a smile.

"Si, Si, like Popeye Senior Mark. The leafy greens will give you strength and the fruit will give you the energy. A powerful energy that will make you vibrate at higher levels. Proteins like meat, dairy, beans, and soy will bring you way down and produce acids. Starches, like we mentioned before will clog you up with mucus. You want your energy to flow freely within you."

"So why do they put the gold in the bread? Bread is a starch right?" I asked.

"Indeed, but they didn't have the knowledge or technology that we do now in 2010. Now I can give you a tincture of the gold. Which I will do now since it came up."

Oscar opened a closet door and in it was hundreds of glass tincture bottles with no labels.

"This is the monoatomic gold broken down into liquid form. We soak it in a high quality vodka for up to 6 weeks. The vodka extracts the goodness out of the gold. I am going to give you a nice supply to take with you. Twice a day, you will take 3 drops under your tongue. One in morning and one at night."

"Okay but what about when it runs out?" I asked.

"That is why everything must be done correctly and in unison my friend. You also need to work on a meditation practice."

"How often do I meditate?"

"As much as you can. Mornings right after waking up is best because your mind is still in a sleep state and pineal gland is turned on. But you also do when you feel stressed and you need to relax. Sit down, focus on your breath, focus on the center of your forehead. Turn your thoughts off. If thoughts come forth, recognize them, and push them away. The goal is to move past the mind so you can hear the soul."

"I understand." I said.

"The more you advance essay, the more things will start feeling different. Your intuition will increase, the bridge of your nose will randomly tingle, and you will begin to vibrate at a higher level. We are all energy. You can harness that energy when you combine meditation, with a high fruit diet, and this gold."

"What about fasting?" I asked.

"Fasting is the ultimate. Your vibrations will rise essay. Of course you may experience detox symptoms too, but when they pass you will vibrate at high frequencies because your body is harnessing the energy. I recommend fasting once a week on water. This will help. But you don't want to fast when you're performing high activities. So pick and choose your times wisely."

"And take the gold everyday right?"

"Si, starting tomorrow, everyday till every last drop is gone."

"Is there anything else I should know Oscar?"

"Last thing is exercise. You must strengthen yourself. Do push-ups, squats, run in place to work your heart and lungs. Get in shape, the strongest survive Chico. It's gonna be a mucho grande journey for you Senior Mark. We're all rooting for you. You're the key."

CHAPTER 25

The Departure

We got back to the hotel room.

"Are you hungry?" I asked Victoria.

"I sure am, what are you thinking?"

"My intuition is telling me to stay in. We were out enough today, we can't be made by the other side. Let's do room service."

"Okay honey that's fine."

"I'm in the mood for pancakes! A little breakfast for dinner?" I asked enthusiastically.

She chuckled. "Remember you're not supposed to have too much starches."

"Yeaaaaaaah....I know. But I can start that tomorrow."

We both laughed, then shared an intimate kiss.

She pulled her head back with her arms still wrapped around my neck.

"Can I tell you something Mark?"

"Of course." I replied.

"I wish I didn't have to leave tonight." She sighed. "I wish I could just stay with you or you could come back with me. I wish that we could grow this relationship." She spoke passionately. "I wish that...I wish that we had the opportunity...the chance...to maybe have a family one day."

"I wish those things too." I kissed her on her forehead. "But you know what? I am so grateful and honored that we had this time to spend with each other."

She started to tear up. I touched her face and wiped away some tears.

"You will forever be a part of me Victoria. Thank you for coming into my life."

She busted out crying and hugged me tight. And then, the tears rolled down my face.

"You know what I found the most interesting about the tattoo shop today Mark?"

"What's that?" I replied as we both scarfed down our pancakes.

"Jesus. He didn't really give any information about Jesus, but recognized my comment about him being a Demigod."

"Yeah, that's true isn't it?" I said.

She went on. "What do you think? I mean, you know more of the background on these Anunnaki guys."

I thought about it….

"You know…I think it's highly possible that a high ranking Anunnaki from the good side got Mary pregnant. This would increase the bloodline like Oscar mentioned with Chavo. This would give Jesus extra powers as he would be closer to enlightenment than an average human."

"But what would be the purpose of having this one person enlightened?" She asked.

"Hmmm…Well, probably the same reason why they build the Georgia Guidestones or made the 10 Commandments. They are concerned with us. They want mankind to thrive. Jesus was all about love and peace. He had powerful teachings and changed a lot of lives you know?"

"Yeah." She said. "His powers would explain him healing the sick and walking on water. Oscar also said that fasting was the ultimate. Remember, Jesus went into the desert for 40 days and 40 nights to fast and meditate. It was at that time he was tempted by the 'demon' or the actual 'devil' himself."

"That could have been a watcher from the other side trying to sway Jesus, but he resisted." I said, "You know it does kind of make sense. When these Anunnaki beings helped ancient civilizations improve, they were viewed as 'Gods' because of their superior powers. Word on Jesus's feats spread across the world. It's no wonder people turned it into a religion. They viewed him as a 'God'."

"What about the father? Who is the father that he speaks of? He says the only way to the father is through him," She remarked.

"Great question. The Father could be Anu. He was the Anunnaki king and was father of Enki and Enlil who were the two watchers in charge of mankind in the beginning. I was told Moses was able to speak to the Anu through golden mist. Maybe Jesus did the same? Maybe he spoke to Anu directly? Who knows...but him declaring that it has to be through him is evident in my mind. I think what he's saying is be like him. Jesus was the example. He ate well, he loved all, he didn't fight, stood up for the poor, he had a mission, he meditated, and he fasted. Pretty much all the things Oscar is telling me to do isn't it?"

She smiled. "Good point honey."

"If it was all true, can you imagine what that knowledge would do to the world?" I said.

"Wow!" She said. "So many people are Christians and wear crosses around their neck, it would be devastating to hear anything related to an alien race!"

A few hours went by. We had some quality time lying in bed. Kissing, cuddling, and talking. It was the most comfortable I had ever been with a woman. But time always catches up and it did with us as well. Her flight was taking off in a few hours and it was time for her to go to the airport.

I couldn't go with her as I shouldn't be out and about. I handed her all the money she needed for the traveling, and I called her a cab. The tears were flowing from both of us. It was a heart wrenching goodbye. One that I don't care to elaborate much on as a write this.

When I woke up the next day...I felt completely empty. Like the best thing that ever happened to me had been taken away. Like I got to visit heaven for 10 minutes and then had to leave. The emotions got the best of me and I shed more tears. But it wasn't long before my intuition kicked in. I had a mission to complete. This was my job. I knew I had an important day in front of me. I had to find a room to rent. This would become my home for a short time so I could hunker down and write a book.

I went down to the hotel lobby. They had they had a computer hooked up for customers. I got on Craigslist and went through the process. After about 3 Hours of research and phone calls from the hotel lobby, I finally found a place that would accept cash payments weekly. I didn't have the luxury or time to go look at these places. I had to just use my best judgement to pick one and then show up to live. I had to keep telling myself, it's only for a month or so.

While I was at the computer, I figured this would be a good time to check out the news. Virgil was adamant about me 'keeping my finger on the pulse', so that's what I had to do. I checked out the Atlanta area. The double homicide case at Mrs. Blank's seemed to have died down a little. It was still there, but you could tell the media was just holding on for ratings. I didn't see my name anywhere, so the other side hadn't pulled that card yet. But I knew it would be coming soon.

Then I went to the Elberton Star. The reporters were doing the same as the Atlanta area, just holding on for dear life to the Mrs. Blank story. And then my eyes saw a headline that sent my body into the strangest feeling I've ever experienced.

"24-Year Old Waitress Dies In Car Crash"

My heart hit the floor, my body started to shake, tears started to come out. I couldn't bear to read the story, but knew I needed to...

It happened around 2:10 a.m. Tuesday on Lower Heard St. Police say an Acura heading southbound lost control and crossed into the northbound lane, driving off road and colliding with a Telephone Pole.

The driver of the car was the only injury. She has been identified as Victoria Guerrero of Elberton, GA. It's reported that she died on impact. She was coming back from the Athens-Ben Epps Airport and it's believed that she fell asleep behind the wheel of the car. Wet roads and speed appear to have played a role in the crash as well.

I fell off the chair and onto the floor in the lobby. My body shook in uncontrollable spasms as I wept. The hotel receptionist came over to me. She could tell I had just received horrible news. She was kind enough to hold me as I cried in a strange woman's arms in a Miami hotel lobby.

A few hours later it dawned on me what had happened. I don't believe Victoria fell asleep behind the wheel at all, do you? I think it's pretty obvious the other side tracked her every move and then ran her off the road. I feel like Hickenbottom manipulated her to come pick up the footage from me knowing that the other side had an eye on her. I feel like he knew this would happen. It was a chess move, so the other side thinks they have the only copies of the footage. My blood boils when I think about Hickenbottom using this sweet girl as a pawn! I wonder if he will show his face to me again.

This incident was an eye opener. It's clear now that I'm in the middle of a war. It's Enki vs Enlil, and I'm supposedly the human that ends it.

This is too much…

CHAPTER 26

The Reality

For the last month or so I've been cooped up indoors writing, meditating, exercising, eating grapes, and growing a beard. I now understand why Virgil instructed me to come to Miami. It's a tourist attraction full of celebrities, tourists, and good fruit. It's easy to get lost into the sea of people. I didn't go out much, but when I did, most people were caught up in talking about Lebron coming to the Miami Heat to play basketball.

Just as I was told, the grapes are powerful. My body is cleansing and things are coming out that I didn't even knew existed inside me!   Black mucoid matter, fluke worms, rope worms, not to mention I've had intermittent rashes and headaches from the toxins leaving my tissues. I've lost about 15 pounds but gained muscle from the push-ups, squats, and cardio.

Mentally, I'm still dealing with all the grief. While I do cry sometimes, the meditation has kept me grounded. Sometimes I see incredible visions of purplish mountains and hear a flute from a faint distance.   And sometimes I see things happen days or even hours before it actually occurs. I guess my pineal is opening. I'm improving.

This journal wasn't easy to write, especially doing it in a month's time. It was difficult to use fake names for people that I care about, it was heartbreaking to recall traumatic incidents, and it was devastating to come face to face with the harsh reality that there is a bigger journey ahead. These chronicles are far from over, for this was only the making of the ELBERTON ENIGMA.

I guess it's time to open up Virgil's notebook and see what's next...

ABOUT THE AUTHOR

Kevin W. Reese is an author, motivational speaker, and natural health educator who has guided and inspired thousands of people to take control of their lives through his seminars, books, and social media presence.

As a sought-after public speaker, Kevin's been invited to universities, health expo's, churches, high schools, children's events, and correctional institutions. He's published two health books, an adventure novel, and launched a series of children's books based around a health hero cartoon named Sunlight Sonny.

Before becoming a health professional and author, Kevin was an unhealthy on-air host at CBS Radio where he interviewed celebrities, hosted concerts, and was known as a "shock jock." A cigarette smoker with a severe food addiction, he eventually found himself on heart monitors at twenty-eight years old. Tired and fed up, he took control back by losing nearly eighty pounds, quitting smoking, and reversing chronic issues. Through his major shift, he became passionate about natural health and healing and followed his calling. After 12 years as a professional on-air talent, he shocked listeners by retiring from the airwaves to start a full-time health practice where he helped clients with arthritis, migraines, eczema, anxiety, stress, smoking, and much more.

Between Kevin's fun personality, captivating story, and presence on social and traditional media, he's making a positive influence on people from all around the world.

To learn more about Kevin and his work, visit his website:

www.KEVINWREESE.com

For daily inspiration and education, like Kevin's Facebook page:

www.FACEBOOK.com/KevinWReeseOfficial

www.ingramcontent.com/pod-product-compliance
Lightning Source LLC
Chambersburg PA
CBHW071253250626
47159CB00004B/1164